Praise for
Muzzle the Black Dog

"A mysterious stranger at a cabin door sets off a series of explosive events in Cobb's moody mystery." - *Kirkus Reviews*

"Mike Cobb continues to evolve as a writer, using his solid foundation of deep research, complex characters, deft application of literary devices, and fluid prose to expand into new realms of historical fiction and true crime interwoven with equally disturbing fictional crimes that come from the writer's (and the characters') fertile imaginations. I am looking forward to what comes next."

Joey Madia, author of *Sherlock Holmes and the Mystery of M* and the *Stanton Chronicles* historical fiction series.

"Mike Cobb's Muzzle the Black Dog is a fast-paced, unputdownable thriller that will leave you guessing until the very end."

Westley Smith, author of *Some Kind of Truth* and *In the Pale Light*

"The pages just fly by in this quick-moving, compelling and stunningly unique psychological thriller about a man searching for answers to a deadly crime who uncovers long-buried secrets about himself and his own troubled past. *Muzzle the Black Dog* takes the reader on a wonderfully wild roller coaster of a ride filled with plenty of twists, thrills and tension. Mike Cobb has written a terrific book – read it!"

R.G. Belsky, author of the Clare Carlson mystery series

"A mystery whose plot will transfix you and whose finish will stun you, Muzzle the Black Dog is simply superb. A stranger enters narrator Jack Pate's life and proceeds to upend it through his bizarrely intimate knowledge of Jack's past. In determining the identity of the visitor, Jack solves a deeper mystery within himself, but doing so provokes demons in his soul, demons he'd been holding at since childhood. Author Mike Cobb provides that rare combination of masterly prose, passion, and insight, in an atmosphere dark and chilling as a Georgia winter."

Charles Philipp Martin, author of the Inspector Lok novels
Rented Grave and Neon Panic

"*Muzzle the Black Dog* takes you on a rollercoaster of emotions and family secrets. The slow reveal is creepy many times, but you still want to read page after page. I loved the combination of thriller, drama, history and mystery."

Erik S. Meyers, author of The Sally Witherspoon
Mystery Series

"Intriguing doesn't begin to describe the appeal of this book's premise: a mysterious stranger on the doorstep of recluse Jack Pate, offering friendship and help. Despite Jack's surprise (he has no need of aid) and suspicion of the disheveled man—who looks more like a vagrant than any friend he would choose—Jack is fascinated. Who is this man, and how did he find Jack's secluded cabin? And why does he seem to know things about Jack's uneasy past?

Just as suddenly as the stranger appears, he vanishes, leading Jack on an odyssey, beginning as a physical search but quickly morphing into self-preservation as reports of heinous local crimes trickle in. Arson and murders begin to stain the remote countryside, and the suspects are few and far-between. Sneaky clues, well-drawn characters, and swift plotting propel the story forward as the author deftly explores the many ways the past affects the present—and how it might endanger the future. I highly recommend this one."

Jennifer Sadera, author of *I Know She Was There*

"A slow burn of a story revealing the power of deeply held secrets. Secrets so earthshaking that Jack Pate questions everything he believed when a mysterious stranger knows everything about him. Moody and atmospheric."

James L'Etoile, award-winning author of *River of Lies* and the Detective Nathan Parker series

MUZZLE THE BLACK DOG

MIKE COBB

Waterside Productions

First Printing, 2025

ISBN-13: 978-1-962984-84-3 print edition
ISBN-13: 978-1-962984-85-0 e-book edition

Waterside Productions
2055 Oxford Ave
Cardiff, CA 92007
www.waterside.com

Of three or four in the room, one is always looking out the window.
And one is outside looking in.

(from Yehuda Amichai, with liberties taken)

2004

1

OUTLANDER

He didn't show up at my door that night out of thin air. Well I guess, technically, he did. But somebody, or something, had to have sent him. Otherwise, how would he have ended up eleven miles—eleven point three to be exact—from anything resembling civilization?

I was awakened from a light doze by dogs barking in the distance. Free rangers. At first, I thought nothing of it. Probably cornered a bobcat. Maybe a fox. Or baying at a barn owl snaring its quarry. It wasn't until I heard heavy footsteps that I knew I had a drop-in. But I hardly ever have drop-ins. It was almost midnight. *What the hell?*

I peered from around the muslin curtain, my passing facsimile of Desert Storm camouflage. A stranger stood at the door, shifting his weight from foot to foot. He saw me. We locked eyes. The low-lying fog that had settled in a couple hours earlier gave him a wraithlike mien. I could make out enough to tell he had dark scraggly hair. Not too long but cutting a mophead silhouette against the light from the waxing moon. Disheveled beard, greying around the temples and chin. I could have sworn I was witnessing an older Eric Rudolph in the flesh. *But they caught him, right? Damn, that was seven months ago. Time flies.* His brother, maybe? No, it couldn't be. The man at my door had two hands—I know, because he held a canvas sack in one and a gnarly walking stick in the other—and I had read in the *Cherokee Scout* that Rudolph's brother had cut off his left hand with a radial arm saw. *But wait…didn't the article say the doctors reattached it? Could it be?*

"What do you want?" I yelled through the locked door.

"I'm here to help you."

"Help me? I don't need help. Okay?"

"Well, perhaps you can help *me*, then."

"With what?"

"Let me in, please."

"I don't know you."

"You don't *think* you know me. But you do."

"How? From where?"

"You're Jack, right? Jack Pate."

"Who are *you*?"

"Let's just say I'm a friend you didn't know you had. Let me in, man. It's cold as the dickens out here."

"Why should I let a perfect stranger into my house?"

"Because I'm not a stranger. I just told you, I'm a friend you didn't know you had."

I pondered whether to let the outlander in. My inclination was to turn him away. To tell him to move the hell on. But my interest was piqued. He knew my name. But how? He had sought me out. But to what end? I decided, against my better judgment and maybe to my detriment, to let him in. Albeit with an abundance of caution.

I grabbed my Stoeger side-by-side. I freed the deadbolt ever so gently so he wouldn't hear. I walked across the room and stood halfway between the hearth and the door, feet shoulder width and planted firmly on the floor. I leveled the gun where I reckoned his heart would be. Dead center. Bullseye. "Come in. It's unlocked."

The door eased a crack. Now a bluster of winter chill jostled its way into the room, blowing the door open so hard it doubled back and slammed against the cabin wall. As soon as he saw me, he dropped the sack and stick. His arms shot into the air. "Don't shoot, man. I'm not here to hurt you."

His eyes were hollow dark caverns. His gaze was cut glass. He looked even more spectral with the fog behind him and the cabin's dim light washing over him.

I nodded toward the center of the room. "Bring your shit in with you."

He picked up the sack and stick and limped across the threshold. A waft of funk followed him. He set his sack beside the door. He leaned his stick against the door casing.

"Shut the door," I said. "I let you in. Okay? Now tell me how you know my name."

"Can I have a seat first? I've been on the road a long time and my feet are killing me."

I lowered the Stoeger but kept a grip on it. I pointed toward the straight back chair near the corner. The one with the fraying cane seat. "Sit there. But take off your coat first. Hang it on the rack by the door. On the free peg. Okay?"

He slipped his arms out of his coat. He hung it where I had told him to.

I walked over to the coat. It was a Beretta Gunner Field Jacket, dry-waxed with a rich hunter brown patina. The kind you can't buy at just any store. There was a one-inch rip near the shoulder. The cut looked fresh, with clean edges. I ran my left hand through each pocket, careful to train the Stoeger on my interloper.

In the jacket's right pocket I found a half-full, crushed-in nonfilter soft pack of Camels. And a strike-anywhere matchbook with CITY LOCK SERVICE, MURPHY, N.C. on the front.

"Stand back up," I said. "Hands in the air."

I approached him. I held the Stoeger tightly in my right hand. With my free one, I patted down his right side, the inseam of his left leg. I switched hands. *Lather, rinse, repeat.*

"Sit back down."

I sat in the chair facing him with my back to the hearth. The light and shadow from the flickering fire danced on his whiskered face. If I had to guess, I'd say he hadn't seen a shower in three weeks or more.

"Do you know who you look like?" I said. "You look just like Eric Rudolph. If I didn't know better, I'd swear that's who you are. Okay?"

He frowned. "Who is that?"

"Eric Rudolph? Where the hell have you been, man? You don't know who Eric Rudolph is? The Olympic Park bomber?"

"Of course. I recognize the name now. I'm not a newshound. And besides, I try not to remember things that don't matter. Selective recall." His eyes darted to the ceiling. "And that Eric Rudolph fellow means nothing to me."

"Now that you're sitting down, will you tell me how you know me?"

"Did I say I knew you? I said *you* know *me*."

"But you knew my name. Right?"

"You have me there, Jack Pate. I know your name."

"Okay then, so how do *I* know *you*?"

"Are you seeking affirmation? Are you trying to control me? Or are you just concerned?"

"What?"

"What's with the verbal tic?"

I frowned. "Verbal tic?"

"Okay? Right? Dependent personality disorder if you ask me."

"What are you talking about?"

"I'm no shrink, but if one were sitting right here beside me, he'd tell you that when a gent says things like *okay* and *right* over and over, as a question, it usually means he needs validation, reassurance. To be taken care of. Not to be abandoned—"

"Do you think that's me?"

"I wasn't through...especially by somebody they love. But other people do it to control their interlocutor, a backhanded way of saying *of course I'm right*. Tricky, don't you think? Or maybe yours is involuntary. Tourette's lite, if you will." He leveled his cut-glass gaze on me. "Which is it for you, Jack Pate?"

Before I could respond, he continued. "If you ask me, in your case, I think you're trying to control me. Fixed gaze, stiff face. 'Where the hell have you been, man?' Dead giveaways. Then again, maybe you just want to be my friend and you don't know how to show it." He paused. "Okay?" An ear-to-ear grin formed, exposing a bright gold crown on number 5. "That was for you, Jack Pate."

"Do you think, just maybe, that my fixed gaze and stiff face are because I'm sitting here, at a quarter to one, across the room from a drifter who happened to waltz in uninvited and crash my one-man band?"

"Perhaps, Jack Pate. But please don't call me a drifter. I prefer errant knight. May I impose upon you for a jet black cup of joe? A morsel? A donut? Anything."

"You don't need to keep saying my name. I get it. You know who I am."

"I just like the sound of it. That's all. It has a bisyllabic crispness to it, if you know what I mean. Okay?" There was that grin again. "See, there I go. You're rubbing off on me."

I caught something out of the corner of my eye. I blinked and stared in its direction. A wisp scampered along the baseboard opposite where we sat. It disappeared as quickly as it had arrived. Was it a field mouse? A shrew? Or just a shadow from the fire?

I turned my attention back to the man sitting across from me. "Did you see that?"

"What?"

"Never mind. When's the last time you ate?"

"Been a while. Two and a half days. A veritable feast. Lettuce, wilted, Bibb. Yogurt, vanilla, low-fat Dannon, as I recall. Peanuts, honey roasted. And some Boars Head deli ham, a week past the stale date. Not what you'd call epicurean, but it got me by. Retrieved straight from a dumpster, behind the Murphy Save A Lot."

"Are you shitting me? That's where they caught Rudolph."

"Why would I, as you say, *shit* you?"

"Murphy's twenty-three miles away. How did you get here?"

"With this thing right here." He wagged his right thumb. "Man in a Ranger picked me up just outside of Murphy. I told him I was headed to a cabin in the woods due north of Marble. He brought me as far as he could, 'til the gravel road turned to washboard. Then he dropped me off. Said, 'Sorry, friend. Cain't go no further. You just go ahead on.' That's what he said, '*Cain't* go *no* further. Just *go ahead on.*' I walked the rest of the way."

"He must not have put you out because of the washboard. Right? A Ranger could have gotten here with no problem at all."

"No, it wasn't that. He just didn't want to go *no further* out of his way." My visitor smirked.

"How did you know where to find me? And why did you want to find me in the first place?"

"It wasn't easy. Would you be so kind as to hand me my jacket?"

I crossed the room and took the Beretta Gunner off the peg.

He reached into the right pocket and retrieved the Camels and matches. He held the pack out. "Care for a smoke?"

I told him I don't smoke. And if he even thought of firing one up in my cabin, he could gather his things and be on his way.

He put on his jacket. "I'm not leaving. I promise." He headed outside.

Five minutes later, he returned. He placed his jacket back on the peg. He picked a fleck of tobacco off his lip and reached for his sack by the door.

"Give it here," I said. "Don't even think of reaching inside. If you do, I'll—"

"Fill me with buckshot?"

"Maybe."

He extended the sack to me.

I grabbed it and placed it in my lap. As he stood before me, I groped through the contents with my left hand, looking for a handgun, a knife, a box cutter, an icepick. Anything he could do me in with. *Out here in the middle of nowhere, who would ever know?*

I handed the sack back to him.

He sat down, reached into it, and pulled out a map. It was one of those old Texaco accordion folds you used to get free at the filling station. With the five-point star on the front. And the smiling man in the grey-green attendant cap—beaming and baring his pearly whites. *Not like the Texaco man I remember. Nicotinian would be more fitting.*

He unfolded the map and held it up with his right hand. Pointed to a big red Magic Marker X where my cabin is. Close enough, anyway. Jabbed it with his left finger. "Here, right here. See. I knew where you were. When I got close, I saw smoke rising to the firmament. I knew it had to be you."

I stared at his left arm, trying to get a bead on his wrist. But it was covered by his sleeve.

When he saw me staring, he jerked his hand away.

"And why?" I said.

"Why what?"

"Why did you want to find me?"

The solitary light bulb hanging from the center rafter swayed ever so slightly. Like a Foucault pendulum. He looked up at it. Then back at me. His thoughts halted at his lips. "In time, my friend. In time."

My frustration must have been center stage, because he looked up at me and, for the briefest moment, I saw in his eyes a blue-devil sadness, a despair, an odd affinity. "I really *am* your friend," he said.

I threw another log onto the fire with one hand, never letting go of the Stoeger with the other. I scooped a generous helping of Eight O'Clock into the percolator basket. Threw a pot of leftover Dinty Moore on the burner. Grabbed what remained of a loaf of week-old New York rye from the Marble Big D.

I pondered my visiting sphinx as he tore half-inch bits of bread from the loaf, dipped them into the stew with his fingertips, and placed them between his lips, savoring them as if they were the finest delicacies. There was something about the way he ate, the way he sat there elfin-like in self-absorbed delight, relishing passable coffee, week-old bread, and canned stew. I found it downright queerish. Slowly, the hollowed caverns became black holes yearning to be plumbed, cut glass became Brazilian blue tourmaline pools. A smile crept up his face. His brow furrows dissipated. The funk settled in.

Back when I was a kid, a down-at-the-heels man showed up at our door one Saturday afternoon claiming to sell World Book Encyclopedias. My father turned him away without so much as a No Thanks, saying *We don't need no damned encyclopedia. That's what libraries are for. Now get on.* Later that same day, when my father was on our roof blowing leaves, he fell off and suffered a compression fracture. He had to wear a back brace for three months and went on short-term disability. Somebody once said karma's a bitch. My father never understood that.

It's true that I had just pulled a gun on *my* visitor. But I *had* let him in after all, even though he showed up past midnight, not the middle of the day. And now I was heating up food for a man I didn't know from Adam. If bad karma was going to come my way, it had plenty of other opportunities to get in.

I leaned the Stoeger against the hearth, but within easy reach. "You know, another man dropped by here unannounced once," I said. "Looking for Rudolph. I almost plugged *him* with buckshot, too. Come to find out, he wasn't official. Just a local looking to get fat on a bounty. Once he realized I wasn't harboring a fugitive, he split."

"Thank you for not plugging me."

"You're welcome. More joe?"

"Please." He held out his cup. "I'm not looking to get rich. I've had my share of fortune. In my day, as they say. But somewhere along the way, I realized it wasn't working for me."

"Where're you from?"

"Same as you."

"Same as me?"

"Yes, same as you, Jack Pate."

"And where might that be?"

He leveled his eyes, not at mine, but at my balding crest, as if he were looking beyond me, to some place far away. "Why, Villa Rica, of course."

"You said you didn't know me, right? But you know my name. You know where I'm from."

"So I'm correct," he said. "You *are* from Villa Rica."

"I never saw you there. But then I've been gone four, almost five years."

"Well, I'm originally from Waco. The Georgia Waco. Due west of there. Fifteen miles, give or take."

"I know where it is," I said.

"I move around a lot now. Up and down 78, mainly. Eschew the interstate, for obvious reasons. They don't take kindly to waggish thumbs on the Is."

"You mean wagging?"

"No, I mean waggish. Puckish. That's me, they say. Recklessly playful. Ironic, in a way."

"Ironic?"

"Yes. Have you ever seen a recklessly playful loner? A man of the road who spends…I don't know…maybe two thirds of his time by himself? Most loners aren't waggish."

I thought about how I could get him to open up. Given that he somehow knew me, maybe he knew my family. Having just met the man, I normally wouldn't have confided personal details. He had shared little with me. But I needed to find out how much he knew. "The wife and kids still live in Villa Rica." I studied his face.

The man's gaze moved from my forehead to my eyes. "We haven't even officially met." He rose to a half-stoop. Leaned in. Extended his hand. "Yardley Bennett."

I returned the favor. "You know *my* name already."

"Nice to meet you formally, Jack Pate."

"Are you going to tell me how I know you?"

"Let's just say you've walked in my Weejuns a time or two. We'll leave it at that for now."

I looked down at his feet. At his leather Woodlands, scratched and scuffed. "But if, as you say, *you* don't know *me*, how do you know I've walked in your Weejuns?"

"You'll figure it out. In time. I can tell already you're a reasonably intelligent fellow."

"So how did you become a drifter? Sorry, an errant knight?"

"Had a wife. Owned a Chrysler dealership. Well, co-owned. In Carrollton. Bankhead Highway. Miracle Mile for rednecks. Sold out to my partner right before the divorce. I tried to make it work."

"The business?"

"No. The marriage. Damned hard I tried. Finally, after twelve years, I left. She took me to the cleaners. But that's okay. I have enough to live on."

"So where'd you go?"

"I hit the road. On a Schwinn American. Metallic blue with handlebar streamers." He looked wistfully to the ceiling. "Pedaled off into the sunset. Just like The Drifter." He lowered his eyes and stared through me. "You did call me a drifter, didn't you?"

I nodded.

"I left behind a lot," he continued, "but I never looked back. As soon as the ink was dry on the papers, the ex moved with the little ones to Greer, just outside Greenville."

"Little ones?"

"Boy and a girl." He placed his index finger to his lips as if in pensive thought. "Let's see…boy's fifteen now. Girl's twelve…wait, what's today?"

"The third of January."

"Thirteen."

"Why Greer?"

"Her sister has a beauty shop there. She…the ex, that is… married a man I call the Five Forks Forty-niner, although I've never met him."

"The what?"

"Forty-niner. Gold-digger. Get it?"

"Not to pry, but—"

"Pry away. I'm an open book. But mind you, I'm a stickler for the rubric. I won't let you skim through the pages to get to the good part. You were saying?"

"How do you get by on the road? I understand the Save A Lot part. But you don't seem the dumpster-diving type."

"As I said, I lost a lot in the split-up, but I still have enough. I'm sure you can tell I'm not a big spender. But I don't always dive. Sometimes I dine."

"Dry-waxed Beretta Gunners ain't cheap."

"You got me there, Jack Pate."

"So, you were telling me what it's like being on the road."

"Is that what I was doing?"

"I thought so."

"On the one hand, I can't say I rue having left. I've met a lot of nice people. Good, solid-as-they-come stock. Hell, I met you, didn't I? But wherever I land, I'm always the stranger. Somehow, I guess, being the outsider was my lot. Always outside looking in."

Or standing at another man's door. "And on the other hand?"

His left hand shot to his side. "What do you mean, the other hand?"

"You said on the one hand. What about the other hand?"

"As I told you, I left a lot behind. Mainly, I miss my kids. But surely you know what that's like. You said *you* had kids. How many?"

I couldn't begin to express how much I missed my own children. How hard it had been to leave them. But I had no choice. It had to have been hell for them, and for Barbara, whenever the Holly Golightly mean reds came upon me. "One of each, just like you."

By the time I got around to looking at the clock, it was two fifteen. "Listen," I said, "do you want to stay the night?" I was as surprised by my words as he must have been. I never would have asked him to stay, but I had gotten only a few pages into the book. I suspected the good part, the important part, would take a while. How could I let him leave with the riddle hanging over me? Without knowing how he knew me, and why he was even here? If he left, I might never find out.

"You'd let me stay here? A perfect stranger, as you claim?"

"It's not an offer I make lightly. But it's late. It's cold out. Where would you go if you left at this hour? And besides, there's still a lot you haven't told me."

"You got me again, Jack Pate."

"I can put a blanket on the floor. And add a log or two. I'll even give you a little plonk before you turn in."

"Plonk?"

"Cheap Carolina Muscat. Yadkin Valley."

2

SEA LIONS AND BLACKBIRDS

I read somewhere that sea lions and blackbirds sleep with one eye open to keep from falling victim. Just in case. I get it. I spent the night aware that Yardley Bennett, a man I had known for all of two and a half hours before turning in, was in the next room.

Was I crazy? There was something about the man. Something that had compelled me to let him in, to let him stay. And it wasn't just the fact that I'd barely cracked the book. It was more than that. But I couldn't put my finger on it.

I slept in my jeans and flannel shirt. With one eye open. And with my Stoeger by my side. Just in case.

* * *

Dawn reared its head way too soon.

I rolled out of bed. I grabbed the Stoeger and trudged into the front room, doing my damnedest to shake off the drowse. I leaned the shotgun against the kitchen counter and knuckle-rubbed my eyes. The faint glow from the embers broke the dark. I assumed that, sometime in the night, he had refueled the fire. I looked across the room through a smoky haze at my visitor. He was still asleep, stretched across the floor with the blanket bunched at his feet.

I flipped the wall switch, turning on the solitary light bulb, now hanging dead still. *Foucault has left the house.* I stoked the fire and put more wood on. I threw a slab of bacon—enough for two—onto one side of the skillet. Cracked a couple of eggs into the other side. Started perking a fresh pot of Eight O'Clock.

Yardley Bennett stirred. His lips curled into a slow smile. I figured the smell of coffee had aroused him. That and the sizzling fat. He got on his hands and knees and grunted to a standing position. He folded the blanket and placed it on the floor in the corner of the room. "Top of the morning to you, Jack Pate."

I grabbed a fresh towel from the closet and handed it to him. "The bathroom's all yours. There's soap and shampoo in there. But make it quick. The food'll be ready in no time."

"Man oh man," he said when he came back into the room. "Nothing like a bracing shower to make a fellow feel like a million bucks. And I hope you don't mind. I topped it off with a splash of your eau de cologne."

"Of course not," I said. "Ready for some grub?"

He sat across the table from me. "So where did we leave off?" he asked. "Last night."

"I believe we left off with Yadkin Valley Muscat. It must have been good. It left you speechless." I grinned.

"No, before that. You were telling me about your kids. Tell me more. Ages? Names?"

"You don't know their names? I assumed you did, since you knew mine."

"You're right about that. I knew *your* name."

"Bobbie's six. Let's see…boy'll be eight next month. Jake."

"Named for you?"

"Yep, short for Jacob."

"You told me last night you haven't seen them since you left."

"Did I say that?"

"Didn't you?"

"I don't remember saying it."

"But is it true? That you haven't seen them since you left?"

I nodded. "But I write. I send money once a month. I may live alone in the woods, but I'm not a deadbeat. I have enough salted away from the sale of my practice."

"When you get right down to it, you don't know them, do you?"

"I guess not. They were so little when I left."

"I know first-hand how hard that is," he said. "I live it every day. Do you think about going back?"

"I do. But she wouldn't have me. Not after all that hap…not after all this time."

"Surely she'd let you see your own children."

I put another log on the fire.

"What kind of practice?" he said.

"You don't know already?"

"Why don't you indulge me?"

"I'm a dentist. Was, anyway. *Villa Rica Lucky Smile.* Like the name? My wife hated it. Said it sounded like a Korean massage parlor. Said I might as well add *With a Happy Ending.*"

I thought back to the first time I laid eyes on Barbara. It was '92. I was a year into dental school and enjoying a cold one at Squeaky's Tip Top one Saturday afternoon. She sauntered through the doorway like she owned the place. She caught my eye. I must have caught hers, because she smiled at me. Not just any smile. But one of those come-hithers like in the movies. Like Lauren Bacall in *To Have and Have Not.* She was in light blue denims and a canary short-sleeve tee that accentuated her attributes. From that moment, I made her my mission. Hammer and tongs.

"It's not too late, you know," Yardley Bennett said. "To get to know your kids, I mean."

"That's a long shot. And a longer story."

"Do you know the Big Dipper?"

"The constellation?"

"No, the ice cream shop. Corner of Fairfield and Louise Lane. In Villa Rica. Over the years, I've traveled twenty-two states. Twenty-three if you count that one time I wandered across the Teton Pass from Jackson Hole to Victor. But I turned right around and headed back. Talk about a godforsaken cow town. But I'm ranging off topic. My point is, I've traveled a lot, seen a lot, and as far as I'm concerned, the Big Dipper has the best butter pecan anywhere. Surely, if you're from Villa Rica, you know it."

"Of course I know it. The wife takes the kids there. At least she used to."

"You mean the ex."

"No. The wife."

"You're still married?"

"She's a good Catholic girl."

"Enough said. You know, you could take your kids to the Big Dipper sometime, treat them to their favorites, get to know them. That's assuming, of course, your wife…what's her name?"

"Barbara."

"Assuming Barbara would let you."

* * *

Yardley Bennett stayed another night. And another.

We talked about a lot of things over those two days.

Baseball. I learned he wasn't a fan, but if he were, he'd "go all out for Charlotte, Triple-A. The Knights, of course."

Cars. Even though he said he'd owned a dealership, he never got into the "sports car fetish." Too self-indulgent, he said. "I left my frat-boy days behind long ago. And I have no interest in midlife crises."

I asked him where he went to college. Wabash. Crawfordsville, Indiana. He said Wabash taught him a single rule. "A man should conduct himself at all times as a gentleman."

Every time I brought up the elephant in the room—how he knew my name and where I was from, how I *supposedly* knew him— he shot me down. "Give it time," he kept saying. "Let it marinate."

I was tired of letting it marinate. I wanted answers. And I was growing restless.

* * *

The next morning, at half past daybreak, I asked him if he wanted to go with me on my biweekly stocking-up outing to Murphy. We'd stop at the Ace Hardware on Highway 64 first, double back and hit the CITGO three miles up the road, then, on the way back to Marble, swing by the Walmart Supercenter to load up on two weeks' worth of food and supplies.

He said why not. Nothing better to do. And he was out of Camels anyway.

We walked the hundred yards up the gravel road to the Polaris UTV. I noticed he had his stick and sack with him. The stick I got. But the sack? "Why are you taking that?" I asked.

"No offense," he said, "but when a man's spent as much time on the road as I have, he learns to take his…what do the people call it…oh yes, *shit*…he learns to take his *shit* wherever he goes. No telling who might abscond with it if I left it behind."

We hopped onto the Polaris and skirred the two point six miles to my Land Rover Defender, which I kept parked in a clearing at the road's end. He heaved his sack into the back of the Defender.

We took Highway 19 southbound out of Marble. Just north of downtown Murphy, we passed the Save A Lot on the right. Yardley Bennett did a little salute.

"What's that for?" I asked.

"That, my friend, is tribute to the last supper…before I stumbled upon you, that is."

"But you didn't *stumble* upon me. You showed me the map. With the big red X."

"You got me again."

I pulled into the Ace Hardware. He said he'd just as soon wait in the Land Rover if it was okay with me.

I picked up a bag of ten-pennies, a gallon of mineral spirits, a grill lighter, and a tube of caulk. I threw in a pair of Carhartt dungarees at the last minute. *A man of the woods can't have too many bibs-and-braces.*

I swung into the CITGO just south of downtown Murphy. I pulled up to the nearest pump and cut the engine. I retrieved the 5-gallon canister from the back of the Land Rover. I would gas up first and then fill the canister with fuel for the Polaris.

Yardley said he was going inside to buy a couple packs of cigarettes.

As soon as I had finished filling both the tank and the canister, I had a sudden urge to relieve myself. I headed for the restroom.

When I came out, I could see across the way that my drop-in visitor was not in the Land Rover. As I approached, I saw a note wedged between the windshield and the wiper on the driver's side. I unfolded the note, a college-ruled 8-1/2 x 11 sheet torn from a spiral notebook. I assumed it was from the one I kept sandwiched between the driver's seat and the center console.

DEAREST JACK PATE,

THE TWO-LANE BLACKTOP BECKONS. MY APOLOGY FOR SLIPPING AWAY WITHOUT A PROPER ADIOS. I'M SURE OUR PATHS WILL CROSS AGAIN.

YOUR FRIEND AND FELLOW SOJOURNER,

Y.B. AKA THE ERRANT KNIGHT

The canvas sack and stick were gone.

I refolded the note and placed it among the other papers and things in the glove box.

I went into the filling station. I asked the attendant whether a scruffy-looking bearded man with a cane had come in and bought Camels. And if he'd seen the man leave.

"I ain't got time to keep track a everbody comes in here," he said.

"But it was just now," I said. "No more than five minutes ago."

"Cain't say I seen nobody like that," he said, "cain't say I didn't either." He shifted his attention to fiddling with the cash register.

I grabbed a *Cherokee Scout* from the stack at the door. I walked back to the attendant and threw a dollar bill on the counter. "Keep the change."

I tossed the newspaper onto the passenger seat and cranked the engine. I pulled onto the highway's verge. I looked south. Then north. No sign of Yardley Bennett. I headed north, driving slowly, scanning right and left along the way.

When I reached the intersection where Highway 64 courses eastward, I decided to take it. Yardley Bennett likely would not have continued north on 19, knowing that I was headed that way. I got as far as Old Highway 64, doubled back along the Hiwassee River, and returned to 19.

He was nowhere. I had seen enough futility in my day to know that I could spend hours driving up and down highways and backroads, byways and shunpikes, with no luck. I gave up and headed to Walmart.

* * *

When I got back to the cabin, I unloaded the groceries and my other purchases. I made a pot of coffee and sat down to read the paper. I unfolded it. On the front page, below the fold, the following headline:

CHARRED REMAINS OF BODY FOUND IN CABIN.

And below that:

ARSON SUSPECTED.

My eyes darted down the page. The remains of a fiftyish-year-old man had been discovered inside a burned-out cabin about a mile south-southeast of Tomotla, near the banks of Rogers Creek. Authorities claimed the cabin had been torched. They surmised, based on what little evidence they could glean from the remains, that the fire had been set about a week earlier. They had begun a manhunt that extended throughout Cherokee County and into North Georgia and Tennessee.

As I read the article, it occurred to me that critical information had been withheld. There was a reference, without detail, to suspicion of a firebomb or some other incendiary device. And to the victim being incapacitated in some way to prevent him from escaping the fire.

If the authorities were correct, the fire would have occurred three days before Yardley Bennett showed up at my door. And if he had come from Murphy, as he claimed, he would have passed through the edge of Tomotla, just as I always did on my trips home from the city.

My heart skipped.

3

DARKLING DRIFTER

"I ain't gonna work on Maggie's farm no more" twanged from the CD player as I barreled down the four-lane on my way to Murphy. "Well, I try my best to be just like I am, but everybody wants you to be just like them."

To my right, the gelid-dew-covered fields looked like blankets of snow. Bleary cows grazed in the distance. To my left, the sun was trying its best to break the early-morning fog.

My mind was battling a fog of its own. After an all-night marathon of tossing and turning— running through the events of the past week, thinking about the burned-out cabin in the woods, wondering why my drop-in had suddenly disappeared—I had finally pulled myself out of bed at five thirty, groggy and miserable.

Two pots of coffee and as many hours later, I had headed for the Land Rover.

I was on a mission. To suss out my darkling drifter.

* * *

I swung into the Murphy library parking lot on Blumenthal Street. I was grateful that the library had installed public PCs. I was grateful for Internet Explorer. I was grateful I hadn't been the wretched soul in the burned-out cabin.

I sat before the computer and fired it up. My fingers jerked as I typed out the name, one hunt-and-peck letter at a time: YARDLEY BENNETT. The screen flickered and churned. And returned nothing, except for one Robert Yardley Bennett, born in 1887 in the United Kingdom.

I searched the Internet white pages for a last-name Bennett in Waco. In Villa Rica. In Carrollton. I found a few. But no Yardley. I jotted down the names and numbers in my spiral notebook. I looked up the Chrysler dealership in Carrollton. Jotted that number down.

The other lead I could perhaps pursue was his ex in Greer. But I didn't think he had told me her name. Or the Five Forks Forty-niner's name.

Perhaps the librarian could help. *After all, she's here to find things people like me can't, right?* I approached the circulation desk.

She looked over her wire rims. A prim smile peeked past her over-painted ruby-red lips. "May I help you?" she asked.

I told her of my quest to find a man who might—or might not—be named Yardley Bennett.

She got a puzzled look. "You aren't certain of his name?"

"I thought I knew it. But I may not. I searched the Internet. I can't find a living person by that name."

At hearing the word Internet, she snarled and let out a little hiss through the ever so slight gap between her front teeth. "Let me see what I can do," she said. She eased a piece of notepaper and a pencil across the counter. "Write the name down, please."

I corrected her. "What I *think* his name is."

She pursed her lips and glared at me. Tapped the paper with her index finger.

I wrote Yardley Bennett in block letters.

She took the paper and walked to the rear of the library. She passed through a doorway and disappeared.

I waited.

A few minutes later, she returned. "I checked my references. I can't find anyone by that name."

"What references, may I ask?"

The smile returned. "We have our sources."

I thanked her and left the library confused but determined to solve the mystery. Should I go to the police, a block and a half away? Tell them about my visitor? Not yet. I considered stopping by the *Cherokee Scout* office. I decided to forgo that long shot for the time being.

I found a bank nearby. I exchanged bills for a pocketful of quarters. I knew there was a pay phone at the CITGO, so I drove there.

I called the Chrysler dealership. No one there had ever heard of a Yardley Bennett. Could he have been a silent partner? I finally got through to the owner. He, too, claimed no knowledge of anyone by that name. I described my visitor to him. He said it didn't ring a bell, that he was in the middle of a "ton of paperwork," and that he would "hang up now."

I called the various Bennetts whose names and numbers I had written down. I got through to all but one. Yardley Bennett? Never heard of him.

* * *

Back at the cabin, I replayed the handful of days I had spent with a man whose name I might not even know. Who claimed to have owned a car dealership where, as it turned out, no one had ever heard of him. A man I had let into my home, had given shelter, had fed, hell, had even shared my cologne with. Who knew my name and where I was from. And who had beguiled me in a way that left me baffled still. Who evaporated as quickly as he had materialized.

Could he have somehow been involved in the firebombing outside Tomotla? I had no reason to believe he hadn't. Or that he had. And I wasn't going to go off half-cocked, falsely accusing a man with no solid evidence.

My mind raced through our back-and-forth wordplay. Was there something he had said—or done—that I had somehow glossed over, that might provide an inkling as to who he was, where he had come from, and why he had sought me out? But every mental trail I went down led to yet another dead end.

I decided to try to get a good night's sleep.

I thought about where my visitor said he had come from. Where *I* had come from. Villa Rica. And Carrollton. And Waco.

Maybe I'll go on a road trip. Snoop around.

* * *

I awoke the following morning more rested than yesterday, but with Barbara and the kids on my mind. I was sure my daytime ruminations about Villa Rica had summoned her in my dreams.

Or maybe it's the season. Decembers and Januarys are always hard.

Sometimes we do stupid things. Reckless, irresponsible things. Sometimes the payback is slight and we go about our lives. Other times we realize, too late, that there's no turning back. No redemption. We ask ourselves why. Why do we do the things we do? Say the things we say? When we could have anticipated, surely, the bitter fruits of our deeds and words.

A hard knock on the door jolted me back to the now.

I ran to the window. I pulled the muslin back. Standing at the door, shifting on the balls of his feet and rubbing his palms together, was a Cherokee County sheriff's deputy.

I let him in. I offered him a cup of coffee and pointed to the chair near the fire. He took the coffee but said he'd just as soon stand.

I had a feeling before he opened up that I knew why he had graced my door.

"There's been a series of fires," he said. "All within a twenty-mile radius from right around here. We're going from cabin to cabin looking for clues. Anything that might tie back to whoever's behind it."

I told him I'd read about the fire and the dead man in the cabin near Tomotla. I asked if there had been other deaths.

He looked away. Then back at me. Said he couldn't go into it.

I asked how many fires there had been.

"Let's just say a few and leave it at that," he said. "By the way, is that your Land Rover at the end of the road?"

I nodded. I thought about bringing up the cryptic reference in the newspaper to some sort of incendiary device. And the victim's incapacitation. But I knew that would take the conversation nowhere. So I refrained.

"Have you seen any strangers in the area?" he said. "Anything out of the ordinary?"

I offered him a refill. I asked him to have a seat by the hearth.

4

VILLA RICA

The Villa Rica Highway cuts a sharp left off US 278, right before the Paulding campus of Chattahoochee VoTech. I took it.

I checked the dashboard clock. It was twelve past eight. I was no more than thirty minutes outside of Villa Rica proper. I swung into the Waffle House for a quick breakfast and a chance to compose my thoughts—or, rather, to digest my windshield meditations from the past two-and-a-half hours. I had convinced myself that I couldn't continue my journey without first scarfing a heavy helping of scattered, smothered and covered. *The last thing I need. But when a man's on the road and the hash house beckons…*

It was Saturday, the 10th of January. I had packed enough clothes to stay a while, secured the cabin, and hit the asphalt before sunup. I had thrown the Stoeger in for good measure. *You never know.*

I stepped through the door and into the Waffle House. The aroma of bacon, of biscuits and gravy, wafted through the air. The symphony of clanging egg flips, clattering dishes, and waffle queen chatter—*order up, triple scattered, double covered*—filled the room.

The place was packed with weekend grazers and short-haul truckers. There were two empty stools at the counter. But I wanted some semblance of quiet—and more than an elbow-to-elbow berth. I spotted a free booth in the far back, near the restrooms. I grabbed it. But I had no sooner sat down than I felt remorse for ignoring the Limited to Parties of Three or More sign, especially when the place was getting close to SRO. I moved to one of the two available stools.

As I waited for my order, I raced through the events of the past week.

Yesterday I had spent much of the afternoon driving up and down side roads between Marble and Murphy, thinking that maybe—just maybe—I'd run into him somewhere. I asked at every gas station I passed. Every convenience store. Every fast food joint. I popped into the diner in Marble and asked there. No one claimed to have seen the man. After countless hours, I had returned to the cabin to collect my thoughts. I decided my best hope was to go back to his roots, to see whether I could connect enough puzzle pieces from his past to at least figure out who he was, how he knew my name, and why he had sought me out.

Then there was the issue of the fires. At least one person was dead. I had told the deputy everything I knew, meager as it was, about Yardley Bennett, or whatever his name might be.

And what did I know anyway? How much of what I had been told was true? How much had been fabricated from whole cloth?

I decided to head south the next morning. This morning.

One thing that always perplexed me about Villa Rica was its own legacy of fires. Almost from the start, the town had been plagued with blazes. The first occurred on Montgomery Street just a few years after the town's founding. An entire block of downtown stores was destroyed. The second happened a decade and a half later, leveling a fourth of the business district within three hours. Then there was the explosion at the old Berry's Pharmacy in '57 that took down four buildings, damaged several more, and killed twelve people. And there had been others since, but none so calamitous.

As I rolled into town, I thought about those fires. How was it that a village named for its very abundance of riches suffered such a streak of its own bad karma?

I was a mere lad of six when I first learned of the '57 fire. That was eighteen years after it had happened, but I was mesmerized by the story. As I grew older, I would ride my bike downtown, past where the drugstore and the other buildings had been, and imagine the flames dancing like fiery tendrils reaching high into the sky. The firemen pulling the bodies from the burned-out hulks. The townspeople gathering around. The tragedy of it all.

Now I was returning to a place I didn't know anymore. That had left me behind. Villa Rica had always been a small factory town on a busy railroad line. For as long as I could remember, it had stayed pretty much the same, with a population that changed little, even though it's less than an hour from Atlanta. A slew of people moved in when the Mirror Lake subdivision was built back in the nineties. But, for reasons I never understood, the town settled back down to about four thousand people, give or take. That's the way it was when I left. Everybody knew everybody. I could pop into the new drugstore downtown on a weekday, and damned near every face in the store would say hello. Would ask how the wife and kids were. Would show me pictures of their grandkids. Would promise to make a Lucky Smile appointment. But in the few years I'd been gone, the town had swelled to over seven thousand and was pushing eight. Strangers had moved in. It felt different.

I wasn't quite sure how to begin my search. Or, really, what I was even looking for. Should I start by just going up to people, some of whom I would remember, some not? *Does the name Yardley Bennett ring a bell? Ever see a strange man hanging around? Used to live here…scruffy but puts on airs. Talks a little different from you and me. Looks a little like Eric Rudolph. Walks with a cane. Claims to have been in the car business. Then up and left. Smokes Camels. Too many.* That was pretty much all I had to go on.

For a moment, I had pangs of returnee's regret. Why had I taken a three-hour trip with so little to hang my hat on? If there ever was a perfect example of looking for the proverbial needle in a haystack, this was it.

What had the note said? *I'm sure our paths will cross again.*

I hit on an idea. I would go to the local library, find a picture of Eric Rudolph, and Xerox it. The resemblance was close enough. In the absence of even being sure of the guy's name, at least I would have something to show people. *Ever seen this guy? Or a close facsimile?*

I parked on the side street off East Wilson. I hadn't been inside the Villa Rica library in over five years. As I approached the entrance, it struck me that the building, with its stark white façade and flat roof, was even more frumpish than the one in Murphy, which had never impressed me much.

Ten minutes into my visit, the librarian—rhinestoned eyeglasses, same ruby-red lips and pursed smile as Murphy—came up with a xeroxed Rudolph. One that came as close to matching my drifter as I could have hoped for, save for the clean-shaven face. "Could I have two copies?" I asked. She brought me another one. I thanked her and left. *Do all librarians look alike?*

My next stop was Villa Rica Drugs, a short drive up Wilson from the library. I bought a Sharpie. I went back to the Land Rover and drew a beard—as close to my visitor's disheveled bristles as I could get—on one of the xeroxes. I wasn't sure when my drifter had last graced Villa Rica, but if, as he claimed, he traveled up and down 78 regularly, he could have been in the town recently. If so, was he bearded or was he shaven when he passed through?

I walked back into the drugstore, Eric Rudolphs in hand. One hirsute. One not.

I showed the pictures to the cashier. She shook her head. "Nope. Never seen nobody like that."

I imagined how my drifter would have reacted had he been there. *That's what she said. Nope. Never seen* nobody *like that.*

She pointed to the back of the store. "Ask him. He knows plumb near everbody."

I looked in the direction she was pointing. The pharmacist—I remembered him from five years ago but, for the life of me, I couldn't recall his name—was waiting on a customer. As soon as he finished, I approached him.

He looked at me askance. "Don't I know you?"

I extended my hand. "Jack Pate. Used to live here."

He stiffened. "Oh yeah, *now* I remember. What can I do for you?"

I showed him the marked-up picture first and asked if he'd seen anybody fitting the description. He shook his head. Then I showed him the unaltered one.

"That's Eric Rudolph," he said. "Didn't they put him away? I think he's in a clinker out west somewhere."

"I know. I know. It's Eric Rudolph. But have you seen anybody around here who *looks* like him, but maybe a little older?"

"Funny you should ask." He swung around and called to his assistant, who was stocking the back shelves. "Betty, who's that fella comes in here sometimes. Looks like that bomber Rudolph?"

She looked up. "All I know's he calls himself Richard. Don't remember his last name."

"Did he ever get a prescription filled here?" I asked the pharmacist.

"He may've. But I can't tell you that. Confidential."

"But you could find his last name if he did."

"Still confidential."

It struck me as odd that, if Betty had remembered the man's name, it would all be just fine. But the pharmacist couldn't look it up in the records. Confidential. *Talk about officialism.*

"Could you tell me this, then?" I said. "Does he use a cane?"

"Not that I recall."

"Does he sometimes wear a brown hunting jacket?"

He shook his head. "If I tried to remember what everybody wears that comes in here…" He stared straight through me. "…I'd drive myself nuts." He turned his attention to the paperwork in front him.

I stood there for a minute while he shuffled the papers.

He looked up. "Anything else?"

I thanked him and headed for the door. I was halfway to the front of the store when the assistant came running toward me waving her hand. "I think I remember his name. Just came to me from the outta the wild blue yonder. Ever happen to you?"

"All the time. And?"

"Peterman. It's Peterman."

I drove back to the library. I took my spiral notebook and went inside. I asked where I could find the local phone book. The librarian retrieved a copy from the behind the desk and handed it to me.

I took a seat at a table near the circulation desk. I raced through the pages to the Ps. There was no Richard Peterman. But there was a Peterson, Richard F. I tore out a page from the notebook and wrote down the address and number. I stuffed the paper into my jacket pocket, returned the phone book, and hurried out of the library.

Ten minutes later, I was climbing the steps to Peterson, Richard F.'s front door. I pushed the button, setting off a tinny and truncated Für Elise. No one answered. I pushed again. Soon, I heard rustling inside and the turning of the lock bolt. The door swung open. And again, just like that morning in the woods, I found myself face-to-face with an ersatz Eric Rudolph. But this time, I was the one on the outside. And the one was clean-shaven. And clearly not my drifter. He was much younger. And shorter. I apologized and was on my way.

I stopped by a phone booth to call the only Bennett I hadn't been able to reach before. *Maybe on a Saturday somebody'll be home.* A woman answered. "Yardley Bennett? Sorry, don't know him."

As I was walking back to the Land Rover, it occurred to me that, when the Cherokee County deputy had visited me at my cabin, I failed to show him the note left by Yardley Bennett on my windshield. I decided I would go to the sheriff's office and show it to them.

When I got back to the Land Rover, I opened the glove box to retrieve the note.

It was gone.

5

LACUNA

It was late—a quarter to eleven—when I pulled into the Villa Rica U-Snooze Inn parking lot and got out of the Land Rover. A catching twinge, the result of a career-ending football injury my junior year in high school, radiated down my left leg. I fixed my step and walked into the lobby.

I slapped a hundred onto the counter and asked for a single room. One night. Ground floor. Outside entrance. Facing the front.

"Gotta have a credit card." He spat when he said it.

I told him I didn't have one.

He looked at me incredulously. "Cain't give you a room without a card."

I slapped a fifty on top of the hundred.

A few minutes later, with a key to Room 107 in hand, I went back to the Land Rover and retrieved my duffel and Stoeger. I saw that the gas canister was still in the back. I must have forgotten to take it out upon returning from my Murphy shopping trip.

Room 107 was pretty much as I had expected. The faded wallpaper was peeling at the corners. A hint of old cigarette smoke mixed with Lysol filled the air. The unidentifiable stains on the sticky carpet left little to the imagination. Its fibers held firm onto the soles of my shoes, making a muted tacky sound as they reluctantly let go with each step.

I pulled down the frayed bedspread and examined the threadbare sheets. *It'll have to do.*

I settled in for the night and flipped on the eleven o'clock news coming out of Atlanta. A breaking bulletin scrolled across the bottom of the screen: NIGHTCLUB IN FLAMES. Momentarily, the newscast cut to on-location. "We were the first on the scene," the Barbie-doll reporter lilted through the TV.

Why do they have to say that? A building's burning down and all they care about is who gets there first?

A club on Fulton Industrial Boulevard, just up the road east of where I was, had been firebombed. The TV screen was awash with flashing red and blue. The building was ablaze. Firefighters and paramedics scurried about. Sirens wailed. The authorities were seeking information about a vehicle that had been spotted nearby before speeding off. A Land Rover. I sat at the foot of the bed, transfixed.

* * *

I woke early the next morning feeling qualmish but determined to soldier on, whatever that might mean. I headed out the door planning to wander around town, poke my head into stores and cafes, whip out my xeroxes. *Seen this guy?*

Then it dawned on me that it was Sunday. A lot of places would be closed. I'd cover as much ground as I could, but it might be slim pickings.

I walked back to the front desk and paid for another night.

As soon as I entered the main road, I found myself heading down Highway 61 away from town, not as I had planned. Something had drawn me southward like a lodestone. While I didn't realize it at the time, it's clear to me now that my nighttime hallucinations of Barbara and the kids, three days earlier, had preyed on me in ways I didn't process when I first drove out of the U-Snooze.

Just south of I20, I saw the Villa Rica Waffle House on my left. I considered dropping in again, but the lodestone told me to keep driving.

At Moss Ferry and Fairfield, I took a left. I could almost make out the ice cream shop, a stone's throw ahead at Fairfield and Louise Lane. The parking lot was empty. I pulled up to the door and got out. The sign said it opened at noon on Sundays. I would come back.

I turned left and continued up Fairfield. I turned onto Abbotsford and pulled over to the curb a block before what used to be my house. My palms were sweaty. My heart pounded like an air hammer. I wasn't sure what I expected to accomplish there. What if I ran into Barbara? The kids? What would I say? Would *I'm sorry* suffice?

I cut the engine. Barbara's car was not in the driveway. Maybe it was in the garage. But she rarely pulled it inside. Maybe they had gone to Mass. But she usually did that on Saturday evening. And I'd never known her to grocery shop on Sunday. Then again, after being away so long, did I really even know her?

* * *

I was awakened by a tap on the driver's side window. The dashboard clock said eleven fifty-three. I squinted through the glare of the midday sun. It was a policeman. I rolled down the window.

"Hey, buddy," he said, "you need to move on. You can't sleep here."

"I'm sorry, officer. I was waiting for somebody to come home. I must have nodded off."

I cranked the engine and waited for the officer to leave. I left the car in Park and looked up the street. Barbara's car was in the driveway now. She would have had to drive past me. There was no other way into the neighborhood. Had she seen me? Recognized me? Had Bobbie and Jake?

I sat staring at the house. The car. The turquoise bike lying flat on the grass this side of the driveway. The portable basketball goal with the height-adjustable backboard set low.

No good could come of what went through my mind at that point. Best to leave. I made a three-point turn in the middle of the street and headed toward Fairfield.

It was twelve fifteen when I pulled back into the Big Dipper lot. I parked in the space nearest the street.

I grabbed my spiral notebook, got out of the Land Rover, and headed to the door. I was halfway across the lot when a voice called my name from behind. I swung around.

There was no one there. Just thin air and an empty lot.

* * *

Early Monday evening, I gassed up and began my three-hour journey back to the cabin. As I drove north, I thought back on the last thirty-six hours.

After my thin-air encounter in the Big Dipper lot, I had continued inside, nonplussed but bent on staying the course. No one at the ice cream shop claimed to have seen anyone fitting my darkling drifter's description—beard or no beard.

I had hit several other stores that happened to be open on Sunday.

And I had spent Monday asking everyone in every store. Everyone I ran into on the street. Even a middle-aged rake in front of the post office brandishing nude self-Polaroids—not something I had expected to see, or ever hoped to see again, in Villa Rica or anywhere else. *Strangers have moved in. It feels different.*

Pay dirt eluded me at every turn.

* * *

It was dark when I parked the Polaris at the top of the gravel road.

I was halfway to my cabin when I saw something leaning against the door. As I neared, I realized it was a package—large, flat, square—maybe sixteen-by-sixteen.

I carried it into the cabin and placed it on the table. There was no label. I grabbed my utility knife and ran the blade down the edge of the cardboard, cutting the clear packing tape but careful not to damage whatever was inside. I opened the package. It was a picture of some sort, but I couldn't make it out through the bubble wrap. I removed the plastic.

It was a painting on Masonite. Of two men sitting at the very table where the painting now lay. One of the men was clearly me. The other was a greyed-out silhouette. On the table in the painting was an unfolded map—with a big red X. And two full cups of coffee. Steam rose from their brims. The fireplace was ablaze. Near the door were a walking stick, leaning against the jamb, and a canvas sack.

I studied the painting more carefully. In the far corner of the room was a black dog. It looked like a cross between a lab and a bloodhound. It was wearing a muzzle—the basket kind. Hanging from its neck was a small sign that read:

Muzzle the Black Dog

I picked up the painting. I felt something on the back. I turned it over. Taped to the Masonite was a note:

For you, Jack Pate.

I grabbed my flashlight and headed outside. I circled the cabin, looking for any evidence of the darkling drifter's return. I went back up the gravel road, sweeping the light from side to side each step of the way. I called out into the void.

Nothing.

6

MUZZLE THE BLACK DOG

The next morning, I awoke with *Muzzle the Black Dog* on my mind. What did it mean?

I lay in bed, fighting the urge to grab a little more sleep. For just a half hour, an hour, whatever it took to snap out of the slumber. But I had little time for indulgence.

* * *

An hour later, I was hurtling back down 19 on my way to Murphy.

When I got into town, I headed to Blumenthal Street. I pulled into the library lot.

As soon as I passed through the door, Miss Ruby Lips looked up. *Oh, it's you again,* I imagined her thinking. I nodded and smiled as I passed the circulation desk on my way to the PCs. She returned the same prim smile as before. I sat before the nearest computer and pulled up Internet Explorer. I typed Muzzle Black Dog. I punched the Enter key. I sat before the screen staring at page after page of ads for dog muzzles—basket, fabric, cup.

I was about to try the search again, but this time in quotes, when I felt a tap on my shoulder. I looked up. It was him. "I've been searching all over for you," I blurted out.

I heard a hiss. Not a shh, but an honest-to-god hiss, like a rattlesnake. I looked over at the circulation desk. My favorite librarian was bug-eyed. I could see her wrinkled brow from across the room. She was shaking her head, with her index finger placed against her ruby reds. I returned the gesture.

My attention reverted to the man standing over me. "I thought I knew who you are. But obviously I—"

"Of course, you know who I am."

"No, I don't. And what do you want from me, anyway?"

"You spied on her, didn't you?"

"Spied on who? I don't know what you're talking about."

The librarian approached. "I'll have to ask you to quiet down," she said. She twisted her face into a lubber's knot and walked back to the circulation desk.

I spotted an empty table across the room. I pointed to it. "Listen," I said to the drifter, "let's move over there where it's more private. Okay?"

We moved to the out-of-the-way table.

"Now," I said. "Where were we?"

"You said 'Spied on who.'"

"Yes. Spied on who?"

"Well, maybe spied is too strong a word. Is lurked better?"

"Lurked? Where?"

"Abbottsford. Your old house."

"How do you know I was at Abbottsford?"

"Were you?"

"Listen." I gathered up my things. "You need to level with me. Now. Or I'm going to the authorities."

"I'm here to help you."

"You told me that once before. And a lot of help you've been."

"Did you like the painting?"

1996

7

I WALKED ALONE

Centennial Olympic Park. Saturday, the twenty-seventh of July. A little after midnight.

The month-long heat wave that had kept the mercury hovering around ninety had finally broken, if only slightly. A coolish breeze wafted across the grounds.

I had decided to come here on a lark.

Six hours earlier, I had gotten home from work. I scarfed dinner, changed into something a bit more in keeping with what I expected to be a rabid throng of jeaned and short-sleeved spectators, and headed out the door, leaving Barbara to tend to five-month-old Jake.

The drive from Villa Rica to downtown had taken a few minutes shy of an hour. I parked nine blocks away, grabbed my backpack from the trunk, and threaded my way up the street, through the bustling crowds, and into the park.

The papers had predicted as many as fifty thousand tonight. I believed it. A fifty-thousand-strong melting pot of cultures woven into a tapestry of diverse tongues. All having come together in celebration of faster, higher, braver. I was struck by the humanity of it all.

By the time midnight approached, the crowd had dwindled to maybe half of what it had been just a few hours earlier.

The R&B band Jack Mack and the Heart Attack took the stage.

And now the band was taking a break. I moved to the foot of the sound and light tower to avoid the crowd that lingered around the stage.

Five frat boys—drunk and rowdy—walked over to three benches lined up in front of the tower. Three of them sat on the middle bench. Two sat on the bench to their left.

An overweight security guard lumbered over to where they sat and began questioning them. That's when I noticed a green military field pack—*are they called ALICE packs?*—lying beneath the middle bench. It was big and boxy. I thought little of it at the time.

The security guard must have seen it, because he about-faced and ran over to where an official-looking man with a walkie-talkie dangling from his belt was standing. The frat boys dispersed. The security guard returned and began asking people, including me, whether the bag belonged to any of us. No one claimed it. The guard then began clearing me and the others from around the tower.

The band returned and resumed playing.

They had just finished "I Walked Alone." Now, lead singer T.C. Moses said they "might just keep going until the sun comes up." He shouted into the microphone, "Now we have a special treat for you."

That's when it happened.

I was no more than a dozen yards away. The blast knocked me forward six feet, and I found myself on the ground with a small gash across my forehead. I wasn't certain whether it was from my head hitting the ground or from a shard of shrapnel whizzing by. Smoke and the stench of gunpowder filled the air.

A slow rivulet of blood trickled down my temple and coursed along the ridge of my cheekbone.

I remembered having placed a travel pack of Kleenex in the outer pocket of my own backpack. I reached up to grab the shoulder straps and remove the backpack. But they weren't there. I swung around to see if it had somehow come off in my fall. But it was gone. I tried to remember when I had last been aware of it being on my back, but my mind was a soupy fog.

A middle-aged man asked if I was okay. I said yes, except for the cut above my right eye. He reached into his pocket and handed me his handkerchief. "Keep it," he said. You'd better get that checked out. May need stitches."

I thanked him.

He said we all better get out of the park now.

I retraced my path through the park, weaving through the frantic crowd as I looked for my backpack. The moon wasn't full, but it was full enough. That, along with the lighting scattered across the park, aided in my search. But I never found it.

I reached the place where I had entered earlier in the evening. I continued the nine blocks back to my car and headed home, with my left hand on the wheel and my right holding the man's handkerchief to my forehead.

* * *

I awoke Saturday morning to a throbbing headache and with Barbara standing bedside holding a steaming cup of coffee. "I watched it on TV," she said. "I was worried about you." She handed me the cup. "This is for you."

I rubbed my eyes. "What time is it?"

"A little after seven." She pointed to my head. "What happened there?"

"I fell to the ground when the bomb went off." I reached up and felt the adhesive patch above my brow. "Did I put that on or did you?"

"You must have," she said. "I tried my best to stay awake, but I fell asleep with the news on and was out like a light when you got home."

The TV was still on and set to CNN.

I watched footage from last night as paramedics transferred someone from a gurney to an ambulance. As the ambulance sped off, its siren blaring, I could see one of the paramedics through the window administering aid.

Choppers circled the dark sky, beaming their spotlights onto the chaos below.

The chyron said at least one person had been killed and countless others had been injured.

I tried to recall my leaving the scene of the bombing. I had a blurry sense of walking through the park searching for my backpack. Of people screaming, running frantically in all directions. Why wasn't I?

Barbara brought in the morning paper from the front yard, then she went to wake up and feed Jake.

I yanked off the rubber band so hard that it broke and went flying across the room. There was nothing on the front page about the explosion. I assumed the paper boy had delivered it in the wee hours, as he always does, well before the explosion could make it to press.

I decided to call about my lost backpack. After thirty minutes of telephone runaround, I finally reached the Olympics Lost and Found. No one had turned in a backpack like mine. The woman on the other end of the line reminded me, with a bit of an attitude, that a *lost* backpack was the last thing on most people's minds.

Barbara came back into the room. "You need to start getting ready."

"For what?"

She put on that twisted face she always gets when I say something that perturbs her. "Jake's baptism? Remember?"

"But today's Saturday."

Her face twist became a gnarl. "I know it's Saturday. It's also the day we meet with Father Timothy before the baptism tomorrow."

I knew that. But somehow, I didn't. Had the fog in my mind become so thickened that I failed to remember something as significant as the lead-up to my own son's christening? While the observance meant little to me, I knew it meant the world to Barbara. And maybe someday to Jake.

On the way home from the church, we swung by the Twin Dees Minimart. I went in and picked up a later edition of the paper. The headline screamed in three-inch all-caps bold: PARK EXPLOSION.

I scoured all five pages of coverage. Again. And again. On page 9, there was a map of the park. The map had a starburst with a big black callout: EXPLOSION. And a circle: DEAD AND INJURED.

I squinted and leaned into the paper. I could have sworn I saw a stick figure of my survivor self. Standing at the circle's edge. Calling out to my reader self, *I am here.*

* * *

Early Sunday morning, I stood before the bathroom mirror, my gaze fixed on the bandage on my forehead. The white gauze, once clean and crisp, now bore a faint rust-colored stain where a small spot of blood had seeped through. I reached up tentatively, my fingers brushing the edges of the tape, feeling the tenderness of my skin beneath. I peeled the edges of the tape away from my skin, wincing as the adhesive tugged at stray hairs. Slowly, I lifted the bandage, revealing the cut beneath, still oozing a faint trace of blood. I reached for a tissue, pressing it gently against the wound until the bleeding slowed. I applied a small dab of Neosporin and replaced the bandage with a fresh one.

My image in the mirror stared back at me. More presentable for Jake's baptism, but still a bit of a harried wreck.

Later that day, I watched with skepticism as Father Timothy sprinkled the water over Jake's head. How could a ceremony that held so much import for others be so foreign and suspect to me?

Did I betray my doubts by standing there, watching my white-robed baby squirm and flinch to shake off the cold driblets? Was I being disingenuous? Was the sense of reverence and solemnity that filled the church just so much nonsense? It didn't matter. This was his day. And Barbara's day.

I felt alone standing before the marble font. Surrounded by pomp and circumstance. Surrounded by believers. Surrounded by shit I didn't understand and didn't want to understand.

In the stone-cold silence of the drive home, my mind wandered off to the dark place. I thought back to my own childhood. I don't remember coming into this world. I don't remember a water sprinkling by a priest on high. I don't remember the first recollection of my being.

But I *do* remember my mother's frequent utterances whenever my actions disturbed her. Was it some sort of involuntary reaction, not unlike Barbara's twisted face?

Mama's words are indelible. "Where did good little Jack go," she would say. "Make bad Jack go away."

Is that how the unraveling began?

2004

8

RUNAROUND

The man I knew only as Yardley Bennett splayed his palms on the table and set his gaze on me. "Why don't we...what do the plebs say? Why don't we blow this joint?"

"I'm not going anywhere with you until you level with me."

"Remember what I told you the night we met?"

"Refresh my memory."

"I said then and I'm saying it now. I'm an open book."

"If you're an open book, there sure are a lot of blank pages."

"They aren't blank. You just need to open your eyes. And when you do, it's up to you to glean fact from fiction. Have you ever noticed how every play Shakespeare wrote hinged on lies? Even the ones about the Henrys."

I hadn't read Shakespeare since college, but as I thought back, I remembered that most of his plays were, indeed, full of deception.

As You Like It and *Twelfth Night* came to mind. *Othello. Romeo and Juliet.* I wasn't sure about the bard's histories, though.

"I *chose* to read Shakespeare," I said. "Eyes wide open. I didn't *choose* to invite *you* into my reality."

"You got me there, Jack Pate." He leaned back and grinned. "Problem is, if I set out to tell you the truth, I'll have to lie."

I scratched my head. "What?"

"Not because I want to, but because I can't help it. It's in my nature."

I said he was fortunate that I hadn't turned him in already. I told him about the deputy showing up at my door and quizzing me on the Tomotla fire. "I filled him in about you. But I said I had no idea where you were. Now I do." I was about to get up and leave when he reached over the table and grabbed my forearm. "Don't do it, Jack. I'll talk. Just not here."

Ruby Lips looked up as I left the library, shook her head, and let out a *tsk.* I assumed Yardley Bennett was following behind, but I didn't look back.

When I reached the curb, he called out. "You never told me whether you like the painting."

I swung around. I was about to respond when I looked up and saw Ruby Lips standing just inside the library door. Then she disappeared.

I turned my attention back to my puzzler. "What's with the greyed-out silhouette? And the black dog?"

"You're of keen mind, Jack Pate. Read the book and the grey goes away. And as for the black dog, that's a topic for another—"

"I know. Another time. *In time, my friend. In time.* You've said that before. Well, I'm sick of *in time.*"

"Patience is a virtue that I fear has escaped you. Take it from me, without it, your life will be cut short."

I ignored his comment and headed to the Land Rover.

He followed me.

I didn't want to lose him again. But I was damned sure not taking him back to my cabin. "Tell you what I'll do. You said you'd talk, just not here. Right?"

"There you go again. *Right?*" Number 5 sparkled in the mid-morning light. "Yes, I said I'd talk."

"No bullshit. Right?"

"Did Willie Shake produce *bullshit*, as you call it? Au contraire."

"Don't keep trying to manipulate me."

He lit a Camel and flicked the lighted match onto the asphalt. He took a deep drag. Blew a ring. "What *is* manipulation, anyway? Isn't that what we all do? Every day? To get what we want? You're a learned man. Surely, you've read Hobbes."

It was obvious we were getting nowhere standing in the parking lot. "Hungry? I'll buy you a meal."

"A bona fide sit-down meal, right? Not some drive-by glop."

My first thought was what right does a roving dumpster diver have to be choosy in the face of a free meal. But I chose not to go there. "I think you mean drive-through, but regardless, I'm not talking McDonalds. Just to make it clear, though, I'm not talking Ruth's Chris either."

"You have a deal."

We found a little diner off Highway 19 just south of town. We took the booth farthest from the door. Yardley Bennett sat across from me.

I looked up from the menu and caught him staring at my forehead.

"I hadn't noticed the scar before," he said. "Above your brow line."

"Oh that. Long story."

"We have all day. I cleared my calendar just for you."

"That was generous of you." I told him about my visit to the park the night of the Olympic Park bombing. About my falling to the ground from the blast. Losing my backpack. Driving home with a stranger's handkerchief pressed against my forehead.

"I was there, too," he said. "In the park that night. Just another face in the crowd. Like you.

"You're shitting me."

"There you go again. Shit is a verb only in the scatological sense. I don't believe that's what you're implying. Because if you are—"

"How close were you to the bomb when it went off?"

"Close enough."

I didn't know what to make of what I was hearing. I didn't believe he had really been there. "Who was playing when the bomb went off?"

He stroked his chin and looked to the ceiling as if in deep thought. "I don't know the run-of-the-mill fan bands very well. Not my style. Me? I'm a Montovani man."

I continued to grill him, but I kept getting the runaround. I changed the subject. "How did you know I was in Abbotsford this past Sunday?"

"I didn't know with certainty. Chalk it up to keen intuition, I guess. Sometimes, things just come to me."

"A nightclub on Fulton Industrial was firebombed. Did you hear about that?"

"I read it in the paper."

"*What* paper?"

"I don't remember what paper. Why does it matter?"

"We're talking three days ago, and you can't remember where you read it?"

He said he felt like a defendant in the Nuremberg trials.

I brought the conversation back around to the Tomotla fire. "When you showed up at my cabin that night, you said you had trekked all the way from Murphy, right?"

"In not so many words, but that's what I said."

"Tomotla's what, five miles or so from Murphy?"

"If you say so."

I told him that, as best the authorities could tell, the Tomotla firebombing had occurred several days prior to his showing up at my place. They thought it may have happened on New Year's Eve. I asked him what he'd been doing on New Year's Eve.

He did the chin stroke again. "Let's see. New Year's Eve. Best I recall, I was sitting with my back against the lee side of a dumpster, celebrating with the dregs of a Mogen David. And nursing a smoke. You?"

"I was alone at my cabin. With a roaring fire and a glass of Yadkin Valley Muscat."

9

RANGER

After having said no damned way, I decided to let Yardley Bennett come back to the cabin with me. After all, he was my bird in the hand. I didn't want him here, but I hated the thought of losing contact with him again.

We parked the Land Rover at the clearing, piled our things into the Polaris, and headed to the cabin.

The note tacked to the door said to call the Cherokee County sheriff's office at my earliest convenience.

Yardley Bennett's flinch told me he had made out what the note said at the same time I did.

I removed the note from the door and ushered him inside.

"Mighty kind of you, Jack Pate, for inviting me back." He pointed to the note in my hand. "What are you planning to do with that?"

I told him I was going to call them back, of course. Wasn't that the proper thing to do?

"I wouldn't if I were you," he said. "At least not yet."

"Why not?"

"Give it awhile. Let it simmer in the pot. They're not going anywhere. Patience, remember?"

I told him I had a hunch the sheriff's request was related to the rash of fires in the area.

His eyebrows rose, curved and high. "Fires? There've been more than one?"

"More than a few. At least that's what I'm told. To my knowledge, only one begot a dead man."

"But you don't *know* that, do you?"

"No, I don't."

I walked across the room and reached for the phone.

"I'm going outside for a smoke," he said.

I dialed the number on the note.

The woman who answered told me to hold for a minute. Then a man came on the line. He said he was the same deputy who had stopped by my place and left the note. He asked if I'd be around later that evening. He needed to pay me another visit. I said sure and, "by the way, remember that man I told you about before? He came back. He's here now."

When I got off the phone, my house guest hadn't come back in. I walked outside but didn't see him anywhere. I called out for him.

I walked back inside and noticed that his sack and cane were gone. He must have grabbed them and scooted out while I was dialing the sheriff's office.

I ran back outside and combed the perimeter of the cabin. I sprinted up the gravel road and jumped onto the Polaris. I drove the two point six miles to the clearing where the Land Rover resides, calling his name and scanning left and right along the way.

The sun had set, and the free rangers had returned by the time the sheriff's deputy arrived. As I suspected, he said he wanted to ask me some more questions about the fires.

"Where's your friend?" he said.

"He's not my friend. He's as much a stranger today as he was when I first laid eyes on him. He disappeared when I was on the phone with you."

I described Yardley Bennett to the deputy, but I warned him, "That may not be his real name."

He then asked if I'd ever heard of a Stanley Jacobs.

I said yes, I knew him. In another place and time, he would have been what you'd call a rag-and-bone man. "Drives a dilapidated Ford pickup. Comes around from time to time trying to sell me shit. Once he offered me a toilet seat with a broken hinge for five dollars. Another time, he tried to sell me a bundle of kindling and a bag of fatwood, as if I needed such things here in the middle of a forest."

"How well did you know him?"

"Did?"

"He was the one killed in the Tomotla blaze. His body was charred to a crisp. If it hadn't been for the dental records—"

"It wasn't his cabin?"

"No. Best we can make out, he was a squatter. Nobody's lived in that cabin 'cept him for, I'd say, four or five years. When did you last see him?"

I said I didn't remember exactly, but it was sometime in late December.

"Ever visit him? At the cabin?"

"Twice. Once to take him a sack of tomatoes I'd bought for him in Marble. Then another time when his truck broke down and I gave him a ride home."

"When was that?"

"The last time I saw him, I think."

"What did you say he drove?"

"A Ford pickup. Old. Maybe early '80s."

"Where did it break down?"

"About a mile down the highway."

The deputy said they had found the truck, but it wasn't just a mile down the highway. It was parked behind the Murphy Save A Lot.

"That's odd. I can't imagine how it could have ended up there."

"We're trying to figure that out, but as soon as we saw the blue-and-white '83 Ford Ranger with the expired North Carolina plates and the Don't Tread on Me bumper sticker, we knew we'd found the truck."

"It was a Ranger? I guess I'd forgotten that."

"Yep. The only reason we knew what to look for is because the fellow that lives in the next cabin over from the burned out one described it for us. Nosy fellow. The way he tells it, he pretty much sees all the comings and goings in those parts. He told us a lot."

The sheriff's deputy returned to the subject of my visitor. Exactly when did he first show up? Where had he come from? Did he say where he was headed? Why had he ended up at *my* cabin in the middle of the woods?

I told him everything I knew.

He then asked more questions about me. I told him about the divorce, selling my business, leaving everything behind for the North Carolina woods. But I didn't tell him everything. No reason to get into the whys and wherefores behind it all. Besides, he didn't ask.

The deputy said he had all he needed from me for now, but he might want me to come down to Murphy for more questioning, seeing as I may have been one of the last people to see Stanley Jacobs alive. Plus, they might want to have their sketch artist sit with me to produce a likeness of my visitor.

The deputy had been gone for no more than five minutes when it occurred to me that I had never brought in the 5-gallon fuel canister when I returned from my recent trips. I grabbed a flashlight and headed to the top of the gravel road.

I jumped onto the Polaris and took off toward the clearing where my Land Rover was parked. As I neared the clearing, I could barely make out a figure lurking near the Land Rover, circling it, examining the license plate. It was the sheriff's deputy. As soon as he saw me, he scurried to his car and sped away.

1978

10

GOOD JACK, BAD JACK

Venga adento ahora, Jack.

Whenever the weekend sun decided it was time to go to sleep for the night, and I heard those words thundering from the back stoop, I knew it was time to hightail it home. That was all it took to get my legs going as fast as they could. Just like the road runner in the coyote's sights. Only in my case, nobody was doing the chasing, but I knew if I didn't get home *now*, Mama would start yelling *where did Good Jack go*. Always in English. For sure, she wanted *that* to come through loud and clear. Then Daddy would have my hide before Good Jack ever had a chance to show his face.

Mama yelled a lot. She said it was because of the Puerto Rican in her. Come to think of it, most of the time when she yelled the loudest, she did it in Spanish, except for the *Good Jack, Bad Jack* thing.

When she got going with the *está*s and the *hijo*s and the *vamose*s, I couldn't understand most of it. Except I knew *venga adento*. And *ahora*. And *tu padre está borracho otra vez*. I didn't know exactly what those words meant, but I sort of figured it out because she said it whenever Daddy would get high on the bottle and end up going mean on her and me.

Bad Jack. Bad, bad Jack, she would call out whenever I misbehaved. *Where did Good Jack go?* Scurrying around and flailing her arms, she would pretend-search every nook and cranny, checking under beds, behind curtains, in the closets, as if I weren't standing right there as plain as day. Then, at some point, after Daddy had used the belt, and I had finally apologized or made up for whatever I'd done wrong, she would cradle me in her arms, grateful that Good Jack had returned, hoping he'd never leave again.

* * *

Sometime that summer, Sparky Brown and I rode our bikes downtown to the Villa Rica library. We parked our matching Schwinn Sting-Rays at the bike rack out front and went inside. Miss Thackston, the librarian, looked up when we walked in. "Can I help you, Jack?" Everybody in Villa Rica knew everybody, so the fact she knew my name didn't surprise me.

"We're looking for stuff about that big explosion downtown. The one in 1957."

"We *are*, are we?" She looked at me funny. "That's quite weighty material for an eight-year-old."

"Almost nine," I said. "And anyway, my daddy's told me all about it. He's with the Atlanta fire department." I puffed up a little bit when I said that last part.

Miss Thackston went back into the stacks and returned with a bunch of things. An old issue of the *Douglas County Sentinel* from the day after the explosion happened. The *Atlanta Constitution* from the same day. A copy of *The History of Villa Rica*, written by a woman named Anderson. She laid them on the table before me. "Do your parents know you're doing this?"

Bad Jack jabbed his left fingernail so hard into that V on Good Jack's right hand, between his index and middle fingers, that I thought I'd scream out right then and there in the library. "Of course, they do." I lied.

After Miss Thackston walked away, letting Sparky and me be, I stared at the picture on the front page of the county paper. Flames ripped through the air. A cloud of smoke billowed up to the heavens. It was so dense you couldn't see the sky through it. It reminded me of the atom bombs I'd learned about in school. Bricks and broken glass were everywhere. Telephone poles were snapped. A crowd of people had gathered beside the railroad track that runs along Montgomery Street. There were ambulances. The Villa Rica fire truck. As I sat there, staring at the picture, I could hear the people's screams and shouts. I could smell the smoke. I reached out and touched the picture. Sparky did, too. It was like we were right there in the middle of it all.

Almost the whole front page of the Atlanta paper was about the explosion. It showed a picture of rescuers and firemen lining the roof of the burned-out building.

I read that there was a dentist office over the drugstore. When the blast happened, a boy, just three years older than me now, was sitting in the dentist's chair getting a crown on one of his teeth. The paper said he was looking forward to having his picture taken with his high school football team and wanted to be able to smile big for the camera.

I returned the things to Miss Thackston with a "Thank you, Ma'am. I may need 'em again sometime."

She just tightened her lips and shook her head.

Outside, I asked Sparky if he wanted to ride over there.

"Ride over where?"

"Over to where the explosion happened."

"I don't want to, Jack. Ain't nothin' to see there, anyway. After all this time."

"Aw c'mon, Sparky. We can imagine, can't we?"

I ended up biking over to Montgomery Street by myself. If Sparky didn't want to join me, that was his problem. He could be a spoilsport all day. I didn't care.

I pulled up to the curb and got off my bike. I lifted it onto the sidewalk in front of where the drugstore had been and flipped the kickstand with my foot.

A big brick building had been built where Berry's Pharmacy used to be. I looked around for a sign or something, anything that would tell about what happened in '57. There was nothing. I wondered whether the people walking by even knew about the explosion. The people who died. The boy.

It was almost *vuelve a casa* time when I turned into the driveway and coasted to a stop. I got off my bike and ran inside. My mother was standing in the kitchen doorway, aproned and bristly, with her hands on her hips and a scowl on her face. "Where have you been, young man?"

Bad Jack spoke, knowing that, if he could pull it off, just like he did with Miss Thackston, Mama would never even know Bad Jack was in the room. "I was at the library. Studying my science."

"Where's your book bag?"

"Um, I forgot to take it."

"Tell me what you studied without your textbook."

"Um."

"Miss Thackston from the library called. Said you were mighty curious about things an eight-year-old boy shouldn't be concerned with."

I didn't know what to say except "Almost nine."

"Earnest," she called into the other room. "Get in here. And bring your strap." That's what she calls Daddy's belt.

As I lay in bed that night, I could still hear Mama running around the house. *Bad Jack. Bad, bad Jack.*

My limbs and backside ached from the belting I had gotten. In the dark of my bedroom, I could still see the rage in Daddy's eyes. Smell the liquor on his breath. The way his whole body shook when he whipped me.

Then I pictured Mama cradling me.

Daddy wasn't a bad person. He just had a problem. When he wasn't drinking, he did good things for people. I remembered when, earlier in the year, he helped try to put out that big movie theater fire in Atlanta. The day after the fire, I'd been the first out our front door. I ran to the bushes where the paperboy usually ended up tossing the Atlanta paper. He always tucked the end of the paper in on itself so he could throw it a long way. I untucked the paper, my hands trembling. The headline read FLAMES DESTROY LOEW'S THEATER. There was a picture of the flames leaping from the roof. Smoke everywhere. You couldn't see any people in that picture, but a few pages inside, there were pictures of firemen. I looked for Daddy in the pictures, but I didn't see him anywhere.

It was a huge fire. Bigger than Berry's Pharmacy. The paper said they thought somebody did it on purpose. It said eight people were hurt. I never found out whether anybody died. Daddy didn't want to talk about it.

2004

11

DISTANT AND NOT SO DISTANT

I watched the sheriff's deputy disappear into the dark void. I grabbed the gas canister from the Land Rover and headed back down the road in the Polaris. After parking and topping off the tank, I lugged the half-empty canister back to the cabin and deposited it next to the cabin door.

As soon as I opened the door and crossed the threshold, a chill, far colder than the night air, enveloped me. I slammed the door shut and locked it tight.

Shadows from the fire danced on the walls.

My eyes were drawn to the light bulb above me. Foucault was back.

Then to the picture leaning against the wall in the far corner of the room. The black dog glowered at me from the picture's depths.

I thought I heard a whisper, too faint to decipher, coming from somewhere in the cabin.

Had Yardley Bennett returned? Had he been lurking in the brush all along? Had he perhaps slipped through the door while I was up the road? I had been outside ten minutes at most.

I ran into the bedroom. I got on my hands and knees and peered beneath the bed. I searched the closet. Behind the shower curtain. I checked to make sure the windows were secured.

A draft coursed the contours of the back of my neck. Warm and moist. Slow and deliberate. Prickling my fine neck hairs. Like someone breathing down my back. I swung around. No one was there.

That night, I slept with the bedroom light on and with the Stoeger as my bedmate.

* * *

The next morning, Wednesday, I awoke with my mind careening among disparate thoughts like a ship caught in a tempest. The sheriff's deputy examining my Land Rover, scuttling back to his car and taking off when he saw me. The faint whisper. The draft on my neck. The Foucault pendulum. The chill. The black dog. I reached for my Stoeger, but it wasn't there. It was leaning against the bedroom wall near the door. I must have taken it out of the bed in the middle of the night. I stumbled, Stoeger in hand, into the living room.

I watched, mesmerized, as the dark Eight O'Clock bubbled up into the percolator's glass filter knob. The aromatic steam spiraled upwards. The liquid swirled and danced in the clear chamber. The percolator's rhythmic gurgling was oddly soothing, a contrast against last night's backdrop.

There's nothing better to clear the mind than a cool, brisk morning in the Carolina woods. And a fresh mug of coffee. I opened the cabin door and walked outside. The steam rose from my cup, curling and dissipating into the crisp air. I surveyed the mountain laurels and rhododendrons, the pines and spruces holding court along the clearing's edge and beyond.

I climbed the hundred yards to where the Polaris was parked and sat in solitude in the driver's seat. The woods were quiet, save for the distant drumming of a woodpecker and the predator call of a black-capped chickadee. Soon, other chickadees and nuthatches joined in, punctuating the relative calm with a cacophony of warnings.

On my walk back down the road, something shiny at the gravel's edge caught my eye. It intermittently glistened in the morning sun. As I drew nearer, I saw it was a small token. I bent down and picked it up. On the side facing up was a man crouched on a bike. Along the token's edge, the words: ATLANTA 1996 CYCLING. And the Olympic torch. I turned the token over. On the back, USA and the interlocking rings. Where had it come from, I wondered. Had I dropped it? But I didn't remember it ever being in my possession. I placed it in my pocket and headed back to the cabin.

My eyes fell on the spot beside the door where I thought I had placed the gas canister last night. It was gone. Was I mistaken? Was my memory failing? Had I not placed it there? I raced back up the gravel road to the Polaris. The canister was not in the back. I mentally retraced my path from the Polaris to the cabin door last night. I just knew I had carried it back to the cabin with me. Had someone taken it overnight?

I was about to pass through the cabin door when I heard a noise behind me.

The deputy sheriff had returned. This time, he had a sidekick. He asked if they could come in.

I said yes. I offered them coffee, but they declined. I offered them a seat, but they said they'd prefer to stand.

"Mr. Pate," the deputy said, "we'd like you to come down to Murphy with us. We have some questions we'd like to ask you. And while you're there, we can have our sketch artist do a rendering of your visitor," he searched his notepad, "Yardley Bennett."

I asked if I could drive to Murphy separately. They said no.

I doused the fire, donned my coat, and locked the door behind me.

* * *

The security gate of the jail-cum-sheriff's office opened with a loud, metallic creak. The deputy drove through. The gate, an unyielding divide between freedom and confinement, clanged shut behind us.

My anxiety grew. Perspiration beaded on my forehead. My palms grew clammy and damp. But why? After all, they had brought me in to learn everything they could about Yardley Bennett and his comings and goings. I would accommodate. I would answer their questions. I would sit with the sketch artist as he limned the man's likeness to the best of his abilities. To the best of my recollection. Then they would return me to my cabin, and my only forfeiture would be a few hours of my time. Anything for the cause.

I was escorted to a stark, windowless, utilitarian room in the innards of the building. The deputy said wait here, that someone would be with me shortly. He left, shutting the door behind him. I heard the lock turn.

The walls, scuffed and worn from years of use, were a dull beige. The lighting was harsh, fluorescent, casting an unforgiving light upon the institutional grey metal table in the center of the room.

The room smelled of disinfectant mixed with old cigarette smoke. Not unlike the U-Snooze Inn. The heat had been turned up so high that it must have been a sweltering ninety degrees, making the pungence even stronger.

I had been told to sit at the table in a hard metal chair facing the door. The table surface was a mess. A giant ashtray overflowing with butts, errant ashes scattered here and there. A six-by-nine-inch steno pad, its bent and twisted coil worn from countless flips and folds. A Bic pen, toothmarks and all. A coffee ring, it's dark and frayed edges smirching the table's grey. All serving as testament to the last grilling that must have taken place here.

Mounted on the ceiling, in the corner of the room opposite me and to my left, was a small security camera.

I waited.

In about fifteen minutes—fourteen by my watch—another man entered the room and shut the door. He introduced himself as Deputy Bailey and sat across from me. He placed a manila file folder, a Marlboro soft pack, and a Zippo lighter on the table. He tapped a cigarette partially out of the pack and offered it to me.

I declined.

He said he'd be back and left with the ashtray.

He returned and sat back down, placing the ashtray, now empty, next to the manila folder. Holding a Marlboro between his thumb and finger, he tapped it three times against the table surface, lit it, and took a long drag.

"Do you know why you're here?" he asked.

"I don't know the man that well," I said. "He claims to be Yardley Bennett. I'm here to help any way I can."

He opened the folder with his free hand and pulled out a photograph. He pushed it across the table. "Recognize this?"

I studied the photo. It was a picture of a red gas canister with the words PROPERTY OF J. PATE on the side. "It's my gas can. It disappeared from my property sometime between midnight and this morning."

He told me there had been another fire. This one around three a.m. last night. A cabin on Taylors Creek Road due east of Marble had burned to the ground. The gas canister had been retrieved from the site of the fire.

I felt the blood drain from my face. My body grew numb. Things suddenly seemed out of kilter. "You don't think *I* did it, do you? The can was stolen from my front door."

He whipped out several paper-clipped sheets from the folder. He skimmed the top sheet, folded it back and skimmed the next. "How well did you know Stanley Jacobs?"

I told him the same thing I had told his partner when he showed up at my cabin.

"What do you drive, Mr. Pate?"

"A Land Rover Defender," I said.

"Do you know a…" he consulted the paperwork again "… Merle McBride?"

I said I'd never heard of him.

"He lives in the next cabin over from where Jacobs was found dead. Seems he saw a vehicle fitting the description of yours near the burned-out Tomotla cabin around the time the fire started." The deputy leaned across the table with penetrating, searching eyes. "Where were you the night of December thirty-first?"

"I was at home. I remember sitting by the fire drinking a glass of wine. I'm not much of a partier. And I don't know where I would've gone even if I'd wanted to."

"Were you alone?"

"Yes."

"Is there anyone who could attest to your whereabouts that night?"

I told him I couldn't think of a soul.

He said I was sweating something awful and asked if I wanted a glass of water. I said no, but he left the room and returned with one anyway.

I wouldn't drink it. I wouldn't even touch the glass.

He grilled me for another hour. About the fire last night. About Stanley Jacobs. About the discovery of Jacobs' Ranger behind the Murphy Save A Lot. About the other North Carolina fires. Then he asked me if I would consent to fingerprinting.

I was surprised that a presumably informed officer would even ask such a question at this juncture. But we *were* in small-town Murphy, after all. No poster child for big-city protocol. "Are you arresting me?"

He said no.

"Are you detaining me?"

He said no, that he was just asking me questions. "That's all."

"Well, if you're not arresting me," I said, "and if you're not detaining me, then no, I won't consent to fingerprinting."

He relented and continued grilling me for another half hour before finally saying, "I think that's all for now, but we may need to bring you back in."

"What about Yardley Bennett?" I asked. "I thought you brought me in to talk about *him*. To do a sketch. Is he not a suspect?"

"Hold on." The deputy left the room. He returned a few minutes later. "The sketch artist left for the day. You'll have to come back for that."

"But I thought that was why you—"

"Deputy Reynolds will be back in to get you. He'll take you home. Meanwhile, I ask that you remain in the vicinity of your cabin. Marble, Murphy, you know. Don't go far. Just in case we need to bring you back on short notice."

The ride home was long and unsettling. The deputy didn't say a word the entire trip. I wondered if that was intentional. A ploy straight from a sheriff's playbook somewhere. Do the cold shoulder thing in hopes I'll eventually run my mouth out of fear or frustration or just to break the silence. But I didn't.

My mind was a whirlwind of confusion. The insinuations weighed heavily. Could I have killed Stanley Jacobs and somehow repressed it? Could I have started the other fires and somehow pushed the memory deep and out of the way? I retraced my actions over and over, every detail blurred at the edges. Blurred in the middle. Self-doubt began to gnaw at me. What if there were moments, gaps in time, where I lost control or blocked out something terrible? Something unthinkable?

I tossed and turned all night, my thoughts consumed with my current predicament. And with the past, distant and not so distant.

1996

12

MAKING SENSE

I was surprised when, three days after the bombing in the park, I picked up the paper and, there on the front page, was a picture of Richard Jewell, the rotund security guard I'd seen ushering people away from the bench with the backpack beneath it. The headline read: 'HERO' DENIES PLANTING BOMB. In a mere three days, he had gone from champion to number-one suspect. I sat on the edge of the bed consuming the article word-for-word.

Barbara walked in and reminded me that I had an early patient.

I didn't look up.

"Are you okay?" she asked.

"I'm okay. Just confused."

I had been at the park when it happened. I had watched the man now revealed as Jewell. How he did his best to get people out of the way. How he alerted the man with the walkie-talkie. He seemed serious, sincere. Not somebody who would plant a bomb just so he could find it and be the rescuer.

I'd read about something called the hero syndrome, about how the term was first used twelve years ago when another Olympic bomb, this one on a team bus in L.A., had been "discovered" by a police officer named Pearson. He was a hero, until he wasn't. He was arrested for planting the bomb himself so he could rip the wires out before it went off and be the savior he wanted to be.

Jewell may or may not have been a savior. But I didn't think he was another Pearson. I didn't *know* that, though.

* * *

Three months later, the US Attorney for the Northern District of Georgia notified Jewell that he was no longer a suspect. But by then, Jewell was a dead man walking. Or he might as well have been. His spirit had been killed. His reputation destroyed.

I thought a lot about Richard Jewell. About how, in a heartbeat, a man who seems to do good can become a shell of a man. About the grey line that sometimes exists between good and evil. About how hard it can be to tell the difference. About how good and evil can even sometimes live together in the same person.

I thought about my childhood. About Good Jack. And Bad Jack.

* * *

I once asked myself *how* the unraveling had begun. Whether it was borne of Mama's words. I didn't know. But I thought I knew *when*, as an adult, I first became aware of it and of its impact on those around me.

Somehow, I had managed to make it through the trials and tribulations of childhood, the sessions with the psychiatrist, the pills I hid in my cupped hand and flushed down the toilet when Mama left the room, Good Jack/Bad Jack, the belt. I'd even managed to make it through college and dental school with a heavy dose of oblivion. I was always the outsider, my head somewhere else, even when I was with friends or family. Always looking out the window, like I wasn't there in the moment. Maybe it was my way of coping with my own reality.

But then it all came down on me with a resounding thud. It hit me hard and never let up. I think it started on Halloween night. Or in the wee hours of the morning after. Jake was eight and a half months old, arguably too young to take trick-or-treating. But we had taken him anyway. We dressed him as a tiny Yoda. I went as Anakin. Barbara as Leia. We had a grand time, notwithstanding that it may have been at Jake's expense, given his age.

That night, I had a dream.

> I was Anakin Skywalker, standing on the corner of Maple and Main in a city with no name. It was dusk, but the moon was full. Crowds were milling about. Some poor souls wandered aimlessly, pondering their shoes. Others were rapt in animated conversation. A few were whirling like Dervishes.
>
> Across the way, under a contorted mulberry tree, was a cedar box with the word PANDORA carved on the front.
>
> I saw an ominous figure approaching from a block away. As it neared, I recognized the figure as Darth Vader. He

approached me, and without saying a word, swept his hand in the direction of the wooden box.

In that instant, the box erupted in a massive blaze. Stripping the bark from the mulberry. Hurling men, women, and children into the air. The Dervishes soared skyward like Sky Spinner fireworks, only to vanish upon descent. The screams were shrill. Until they weren't. An eerie silence set in.

Then I saw, no more than a few yards from the tree, Yoda lying facedown in the dirt.

Darth Vader stood over me. "Your works? Or mine?" Suddenly, he morphed into Batman's Joker. He bore a sinister grin, exposing a mouth full of yellow teeth and a shiny gold crown on 5. Then he disappeared.

I bolted from bed. Sweating like hell. Disoriented. *Something bad's going to happen.* But I didn't know what. I didn't know when. Or why. Worst of all, I didn't know what to do about it.

Life went on. Doesn't it always? Somehow, we muddle through.

Nothing of note happened after my dream. No cataclysm. No disaster. I tried to put it behind me. But things weren't the same. *I* wasn't the same. My relationship with Barbara, with Jake, wasn't the same. Barbara said I was testier, more irritable, more fly-off-the-handle hard to live with. More anxious. More depressed. I didn't see it at first. Sometimes it takes somebody who cares most about you to pry open your defiant eyes.

1998

13

RUDOLPH

The Birmingham explosion occurred at 7:33 Thursday morning, the twenty-ninth of January. The TV news bulletin came on as I was getting ready to go to work. The blast had ripped through an abortion clinic, creating a huge crater, shattering windows, blowing out an awning.

The news preyed on me all day. So much so that I had trouble focusing on the needs of my patients. Filling teeth and setting bridges didn't seem to matter much in the grand scheme, although I knew such things mattered a lot to the ones on the receiving end. I did the best I could with half my attention focused elsewhere. I thought what if it happened here? Right here? Right now? I thought of that kid in the chair, and of his dentist, on that fateful day in Villa Rica in '57.

Later that day, I learned that a nail-filled package bomb, like the one that had gone off two years earlier at the Olympics, had been left at the front door of the abortion clinic.

A nurse was critically injured. An eight-year veteran of the Birmingham police was killed. I learned from the Saturday morning paper that the slain officer had carried the '96 Olympic torch and had once saved a woman from a burning building by catching her when she jumped.

A witness claimed to have spotted a white male walking away from the scene of the bombing. The man shed a wig, stuffed it into a bag, and placed it into a pickup truck before driving away. Authorities determined the pickup was owned by a man named Eric Robert Rudolph of Marble, North Carolina. He was identified as a material witness. Investigators were searching for him. They issued a nationwide alert.

Five weeks later, on the seventh of March, Rudolph's older brother Daniel videotaped himself cutting off his left hand with a radial arm saw. He said it was to "send a message to the FBI and the media." Doctors were able to reattach it. What does it take, how strong must the bond be, for a man to cut off his hand in protest against his brother's plight? Not having a brother, myself, I couldn't relate.

In October, Eric Rudolph was officially named a suspect in the Olympic Park bombing. But the authorities still couldn't find him. They thought he was hiding out somewhere in the Appalachian wilderness. Perhaps in North Carolina. Perhaps near Marble.

Images flashed before my eyes like frames on a continuous loop. My standing in front of where Berry's Pharmacy had once been. My thinking about the people killed, including the boy in the dentist chair. Looking at the pictures in the newspaper of the Loew's Theater, the smoke billowing to the sky, and thinking about my daddy being there, but he hadn't wanted to talk about it then or any time thereafter. Seeing the backpack under the park bench and feeling the blast, experiencing first-hand the havoc it wreaked. Richard Jewell, his life destroyed. Eric Rudolph. His brother's severed hand. Anakin Skywalker. Darth Vader. The exploding box beneath the mulberry tree. Yoda.

14

MARBLE

I was on my way to work one morning not long after Eric Rudolph was fingered as the Olympic bomber. I was barreling down Fairfield Road, close to being late for a patient appointment and trying to make up for lost time. Just before I got to Louise Lane, I glanced at the intersection ahead and saw a disheveled man standing at the curb. He was holding a cardboard sign. I could have sworn it said SHOVE OFF. What an odd thing to put on a sign, I thought. My curiosity was piqued. My patient could wait a couple minutes longer. Just past the intersection, I swung into the Big Dipper parking lot and doubled back. But by the time I reached the intersection, the man was no longer there.

I spent the day thinking about that man. About the sign.

When I got home that evening, Barbara was waiting at the door. She was cradling three-month-old Bobbie in her arms. "Jake's driving me crazy. You need to do something with him."

"What's he done?"

"What's he *not* done? He's been running around the house like a little banshee. Pulling things off the shelves. Throwing his water across the room…and at me. He even got into my foundation and painted his face with it. I think he's trying me simply out of spite."

"He's not even three, Barbara. It's not spite. It's what toddlers do. It's okay for you to get upset, but you need to be the adult."

"*Me* be the adult?" she screamed. "Why don't *you* be the adult. Deal with him for once, Jack. Can you do that? Do you have the wherewithal to sit him down and tell him he's being a bad boy?"

Something clicked. My mother's histrionics echoed in my conscience. My daddy's belt. Bad Jack. Limbic red alert kicked in. I grabbed a pot of African violets and threw it across the room, shattering it into a thousand clay shards and sending soil and purple flying.

Barbara said shit like this had gone on too long. She'd had enough.

Twenty-four hours later, I had packed my bags and was headed out the door.

Barbara followed me into the front yard. "I'm sorry," she said, "but it's for the best. You need help, Jack. Help that I'm not qualified to give you. Come back when you've worked your shit out."

"I guess it's my time to shove off," I muttered.

I made the Lucky Smile back room my temporary living quarters, sleeping on an air mattress and cooking on a hot plate. Showering in the evenings at the Y up the road in Hiram. Shaving in the mornings at the Lucky Smile wash-up sink before my staff arrived.

Barbara agreed to let me see the kids on weekends, so long as she was present. But after a few weeks, she started making excuses. I begged her to let me come back. But she said no, maybe one day. I missed her and the kids. I thought of them every day and hoped we'd all be together again sometime.

At first, I hadn't planned to sell the practice. But the little voice inside of me said *shove off means shove off*. I needed to get far away for a while. To, as Barbara had said, *work my shit out*. I was fortunate that, six months earlier, I had hired a young fellow fresh out of dental school. He was bright. He was ambitious. And best of all, he had married into money. It took us three months to hammer out a deal. He'd buy the practice, cash up front and a percent of sales for ten years. I'd stay on for three more months to help out. And he could always dial me up after that with questions.

The day after I struck the deal to sell, I gazed in the mirror as the razor glided across my morning stubble. I felt a sudden twinge of pain. I looked down. A drop of blood fell and made its little red mark on my otherwise white towel, a crimson reminder of my carelessness. Or my preoccupation.

I stared at the crack along the mirror's bottom half, a reminder of two days earlier when, having lost control of my senses, I had thrown a countertop equipment sterilizer across the room. I bent over the washbasin and splashed cold water on my face. I looked up and saw a stranger staring back at me through the mirrored glass. *Loser*, the stranger said. *Nothin' but a loser. What are you? Thirty-five? And you're running away? Giving it all up? For what? Because you can't hack it? Man up, Jack Pate.*

But I had little say in the matter. I had to leave. I knew it. Barbara knew it. It was for the best, she said.

I hung a calendar on the wall in my makeshift quarters. Each day, I marked a bright red diagonal through the square to designate another twenty-four hours closer to leaving the practice and not looking back. And each evening, after work, I would ride by the house, ease my car up to the curb, and peer across the lawn into the windows, hoping to get a glimpse of my family. I had become the stranger. On the outside looking in.

I resigned myself to the inevitable, at least for now. As soon as my three-month workout was finished, I loaded up the Land Rover and headed east toward Atlanta. From there I would veer north.

Something drew me to Marble.

2004

15

DECEPTIONS AND DELUSIONS

Friday morning. The 16th of January.

My father called. "Your mother's dead."

I pinched myself. "What? How?"

"She died in her sleep. They just took her away."

"How did she die?"

"They think it was her heart. You know how fragile her heart is…was. I just hope she didn't feel any pain."

"I'm so sorry, Dad. I'll get down there as soon as I can. Is there somebody who can stay with you 'til I arrive?"

"Bill from next door's here. And the day nurse is coming by later this morning to check in and clean my concentrator filter. I'll be okay. Just get here."

I packed my bag for what I expected to be a week. Maybe two. I included the only suit I had kept from my working days, a two-piece, grey pin-striped number.

As I was loading my things into the Polaris to make my way to the Land Rover, I thought about what the sheriff's deputy had said just two days ago. *Remain in the vicinity of your cabin. Marble. Murphy. Don't go far.*

I went back into the cabin for a quick walk-through before heading out.

I thought briefly of calling the sheriff's office. To tell them I had to do go back home to deal with my dead mother and my emphysemic father. *No*, I thought. *If they need me, they'll just have to wait.*

There *was* one call I had to make. I reached for the phone, but as I grabbed the handset, I froze. Would she hang up on me before I even had a chance to tell her why I was calling? It was a chance I had to take. Jake and Bobbie needed to know their grandmother had died. And Barbara would have to be the one to break the news.

I had a lot of drive time on the trek to Villa Rica.

Time to grieve the loss of my mother, with whom I hadn't spoken in, what, two months?

Time to think through what to do with my dad. He sounded feeble on the phone. There was no way he could live alone, especially with his own bad heart. And with lungs wrecked from forty years of putting out fires and smoking Winstons like a chimney.

Time to ruminate on my own life's journey. From the naif who took Villa Rica by storm on his Schwinn Sting-Ray, fending off my mother's histrionics, my father's beltings, and Bad Jack's unwelcome intrusions, but doe-eyed nevertheless, and grateful that, at the end of the day, Mama and Daddy meant well. To a thirty-five-year-old hermit living in the middle of nowhere, estranged from his wife and children, fending off the authorities and vexed by a mysterious stranger who popped up out of the blue. And now, barreling down the highway to grieve my mother's death, to bury her, and to deal with my father's matters.

I was on Highway 19 almost to the state line when I looked back and saw flashing blue lights rapidly approaching. I seized up. My breath caught in my chest. I slowed down, pulled onto the shoulder, and put the Land Rover in Park. I was about to roll down the window when the North Carolina Highway Patrol car went speeding by. It took a full five minutes for my shaking to stop, for me to regain enough composure to continue down the road. Deputy Bailey's warning resonated again. *Don't go far.* I should have called his office. Maybe I would when I got to Villa Rica. Ask for forgiveness, not permission, as they say.

For the remainder of the trip, I crept along, with one eye peeled straight ahead and the other in the rearview.

My parents' brick bungalow stood quietly at the end of the street, its once-charming exterior now debased by time and neglect. The paint had peeled away in jagged flakes, exposing weathered wood beneath. The shutters, once proudly framing the windows, hung crooked, some broken and others missing slats. The front yard, once neatly trimmed, was overrun with weeds and tall fescue competing to claim the shared space.

I regretted having been so preoccupied with finding Yardley Bennett on my recent return to Villa Rica that I hadn't bothered to stop by and visit my parents. I could have seen my mother one last time, told her I loved her. I tried my best to shove the guilt aside.

I pulled onto the ribbon driveway, parked behind the car I did not recognize, and cut the engine.

A woman whom I also didn't recognize met me at the door. "I'm Nell, the day nurse," she said. "You must be Jack. Your father's been wondering when you'd get here."

"How's he doing?"

"Fair to middlin'. Gettin' by, long as he keeps his cannula on."

She ushered me into the house.

My dad was sitting in the far corner of the room. In the same easy chair he'd pontificated from for as long as I could remember. Its faded mustard yellow, accented with abstract shapes in green and orange, was now tinged with a sickly brownish hue. The armrests were worn ragged. The matching chair beside him was empty. Between the chairs sat a 1970s-vintage TV tray, replete with a stack of newspapers folded to their crossword puzzles, a can of Mountain Dew, a push-down spinning ashtray, and a pack of Winstons. A smoky haze pervaded the room.

His mouth was wrinkled and drawn. His eyes were sallow. The clear plastic cannula looped over his ears and curved across his face, its prongs nestled inside his nostrils. In his left hand he held an active-duty cigarette, its inch of ash hanging precariously off the end. When he saw me, he took a deep drag and then dropped the cigarette onto the ashtray's rotary disc. He pushed down on the black button, setting the disc into a spin and sending the butt into the ashtray's well and the ashes every which way.

"Dad, what the hell are you doing?"

"What do you mean, what am I doing? A man's entitled to a smoke now and then, in his own damned castle, isn't he?"

"You have a cannula strapped to your nose. And you're still smoking?" I shook my head in disbelief. I wanted to say *And you look like shit*, but I refrained. Not the right time or place.

"Did you come here to lecture," he said, "or to grieve your dead mother? God rest her soul."

Nell chimed in. "I've been tryin' my best to get him to stop, but he won't listen to—"

"I've told you before, Nell," Dad groused. "You just do your job and go ahead on. I don't need your lecturing either. Especially not now, with Beverly gone." He teared up.

I settled into the chair my mom would have occupied. I reached across the TV tray and took his hand. "I'm sorry, Dad. I know you'll miss her dearly. So will I."

I asked him where they had taken her body. He said Jones-Wynn. The same funeral home that had attended to my grandfather when he passed. "We'll need to go over there," I said. "To make arrangements."

He reached for his walker and then pointed across the room. He did a little *bring it to me* gesture with his finger. "My tank. On the cart right there."

I disconnected his cannula line from the concentrator and connected it to the tank.

* * *

We didn't return from the funeral home until late that afternoon.

I got Dad settled into his easy chair and went into the kitchen to see what I could scare up for dinner. But there was virtually nothing in the cabinets except for a jar of Jif, a bag of Martha White flour, and a can of Bush's Sweet Heat baked beans. I opened the refrigerator. There were a few items. A package of Polly-O string cheese. A partial bottle of milk two weeks past its Sell By date. The remnants of some kind of casserole. A jar of Vlasic dills on the door shelf. I found a package of fish sticks and three Swanson TV dinners in the freezer. A half-empty bag of Maxwell House coffee sat on the kitchen counter. That was it. *Mother Hubbard would feel at home*, I thought.

I went back into the living room. "What have you and Mom been eating?"

"We've gotten by. Bill brought over a chicken cacciatore a couple days ago. We've been nibbling on that."

"You up for pizza?" I asked. "I can order in."

* * *

The next morning, I rose before daybreak. I had spent the night in my old bedroom, in the same twin bed I had occupied for seventeen years before graduating from high school and leaving home.

On my way to the kitchen, I looked in on my dad. He was sound asleep.

I brewed a pot of coffee and returned to my bedroom. I sat on the edge of the bed and looked around. The room had remained virtually untouched since I left home. Same posters on the wall. Devo. The Goonies. Michelle Pfeiffer. Same maple kneehole desk. Same plastic pencil cup and Tensor gooseneck lamp. My old bicycle helmet hung on a twelve-penny nail over the desk. It was as if, within these four walls, time had stood still for almost two decades.

I looked under the bed, hoping to find, at the very least, a stash of twenty-year-old Playboys. But, alas, there was nothing there but a stash of a different kind, a disparate collection of mini-tumbleweed dust bunnies.

My closet door was ajar. I eased it open, wondering whether my little three-by-three hidey-hole might also have remained untouched. There were several shoeboxes on the shelf. I took one down, sat back on the bed, and opened the lid. Inside was my collection of baseball cards, mainly Braves.

Another box contained old papers from my school days, plus a partial deck of Hoyle playing cards. I was pretty sure that, at one time or another, I had sacrificed the missing cards to attach to the frame of my Schwinn so it would sound like a Harley as I sped down the Main Street sidewalk.

I pulled a third shoebox off the shelf. As soon as I removed the lid, I realized the contents were not mine. Not only that, but they seemed to belong to some other family. On the top of the stack was a wallet-size black-and-white photograph of a little boy, maybe three years old. I turned it over. On the back was a handwritten name in blue ink. David.

Beneath that photograph was another one. Of a distinguished man in a sharp sport coat and wearing a fedora. The man looked unsettlingly familiar, but I couldn't place him. I turned the picture over. There was nothing on the back.

I spread the remaining contents across the bed. An official-looking folded piece of security paper caught my eye. I unfolded it.

It was a birth certificate, yellowed with age. The name printed on it was one I didn't recognize:

David Michael Pate.

Born Dec 7, 1963. 11:23AM.

Crawford Long Hospital.

I quickly scanned down the document.

The mother was listed as:

Beverly Elizabeth Pate, nee Dooley.

My mother.

The father's name was blank.

I began to rifle through the remaining contents of the box. I found another birth certificate, this one for a girl, Cathy Elizabeth Pate, stillborn on December 2, 1960. My mother and father were both listed as her parents.

By the time my father awakened, I was caffeine-wired and fully dressed. "C'mon," I said. "Get your clothes on. We're going to the Waffle House."

I hated like hell to have to confront him so soon in the wake of my mother's death. But I had to know.

I helped Dad into the first available booth.

I placed his tank cart next to the seat and leaned his folded walker against the table's edge.

After we had ordered and the waitress had left the table, I leaned in. "Who is David Michael Pate?"

He paled and began to cough and stammer.

"I need to know, Dad. And while you're at it, tell me about Cathy."

After much cajoling and downright coercion, he confided that there was a girl. My mother's pregnancy had been a difficult one. So much so that she, herself, had almost died. When the baby was born dead, my mother was devastated.

"And David?" I asked.

"Three years later, she gave birth to a boy. But I wasn't the father."

"Who *was* the father?"

He sat in silence, cradling his forehead with his palms. Finally, he looked up. "Some sawbone at the same hospital where the boy was born. Where *you* were born. Not like a plain old doctor, but some kind of specialist."

"*What* kind of specialist?"

"I have no idea, Jack."

"What's his name?"

"I don't remember."

"What do you mean, you don't remember? Surely, you remember something as important as the man's name. Level with me, Dad, for once."

"I *am* leveling with you. I said I don't remember."

"What happened to David?"

"He lived with us for a while. Six or so years. Then she sent him away to live with his father and stepmother. I couldn't stand having him around. Every time I looked at him, all I could think about was what your mother had gone and done. It was driving a wedge between her and me. I knew something had to give. It was her decision to send him away."

I did the mental math. "So had I made my grand entrance before he was banished from—"

My father pulled a face. "Banished is a mighty strong word, don't you think?"

"What else would you call it, Dad? Wasn't he? Banished?"

He changed the subject. Said he never saw the boy again, but he suspected my mother would occasionally slip away to visit him. My father made it clear that, whatever she did, he didn't want to know about it. "Her son. Not mine."

"Why was I never told about any of this?"

"There were so many times I wanted to tell you. But your mother wouldn't hear of it."

"And another thing," I said. "*You* couldn't stand having him around, but it was *her* decision to send him away?"

I didn't know what to believe.

* * *

The funeral was small. Bill and a few other close friends, Nell, my father and me. Barbara and the kids didn't show up, not that I had expected them to. Because my parents *didn't have a church home*—a common euphemism, I supposed, for *lost and hopeless*—the funeral took place at the mortuary. After the service, we piled into our cars, a four-vehicle mini-caravan following behind the hearse, and headed to the Meadowbrook Memory Garden.

We gathered around the gravesite as my mother was lowered into the ground. The officiant from the funeral home handed my father a square-point shovel. My father scooped up a small shovelful of red dirt and, with feeble and trembling hands, dumped it onto the casket. I followed, but with an overflowing heap.

The cemetery workers stood nearby waiting for their cue, once we had dispersed, to finish the job we'd started.

The small crowd began to scatter.

I was helping my father back to the car when I looked up and saw a man lurking behind a pecan tree a hundred yards or more past where the cemetery workers were standing. From a distance, he looked like Yardley Bennett. But he was wearing a boonie hat pulled low, partially obscuring his face. I told my father to stay put and went running across the lawn toward the pecan tree.

Halfway to the tree, I looked back, and Bill was helping my dad into the Land Rover.

When I reached the tree, the man in the boonie was gone.

16

A BEAUTIFUL MIND

I stayed in Villa Rica for a total of nine days, leaving to return to my cabin only after making sure my father would be in good hands with Bill and Nell. He had insisted on staying put in the house for now. They assured me they'd look after him. But I knew the inevitable would be here before I knew it.

On the drive back to North Carolina, it occurred to me that my dad had never said whether David had been sent away before or after I was born. Was my mom pregnant with me at the time? Did they send David to live with his real father and stepmother only after they knew they would have a baby to take his place? Was I a mere replacement, in my mom's eyes, anyway? The word *fungible* came to mind.

* * *

The banging on the cabin door came early the next morning, Monday the twenty-sixth. The first thing I noticed when I opened my eyes was the bone-chilling cold that enveloped the bedroom. I scrambled out of bed and reached for a thick blanket, wrapping it tightly around me.

As I scurried toward the door, I glanced over at the hearth. The fire had gone out, reduced to a pittance of barely smoldering embers.

I pushed back the muslin curtain. The same two detectives who had visited me last time were back. But this time, whatever half-friendly air they may have proffered before was gone.

"Just a minute," I called through the locked door.

"Open up," one of them said. I thought the one speaking was the senior of the two, whom I now knew as Reynolds.

"Can I get dressed first?"

"Open up," he repeated, this time more forcefully.

I unlocked the door and eased it open.

The men approached me. "Jack Pate, you're under arrest for the murder of Stanley Jacobs."

The junior one removed a pair of well-worn handcuffs from his belt and was about to slap them on me.

"Could I please get dressed first?"

He looked at Reynolds, who nodded. He followed me into the bedroom and stood watch as I slipped on a flannel shirt and jeans.

He escorted me back into the living room, where I threw on my jacket.

He had me turn around and hold my hands behind my back. He slapped one handcuff in place, securing it tightly. The sound of metal on metal resounded through the room. He repeated the process on my other wrist. The weight of the cuffs sank in.

"Mr. Pate," Reynolds said, "you have the right to remain silent. Anything you say…"

My mind drifted far away. His voice was just a *wah wah* drone, mere background noise lost in a sea of fear. I couldn't have spoken if I'd wanted to.

They threw me into the rear seat of the patrol car, my cuffed wrists wedged between me and the seat back. The hard, cold steel dug into my skin.

My pulse quickened. I tried to keep my breathing slow and steady lest I hyperventilate.

They whisked me away to Murphy on a thirty-minute ride that I was certain, as soon as we set out, would feel like hours.

On the entire trip, they made small talk with each other, as if weren't even there. I blocked it out. That was fine with me. I didn't want to talk to them anyway.

I stood in the cold, sterile booking room. The harsh fluorescent light buzzed and flickered overhead. I imagined that, somewhere within its aging ballast, a tired capacitor clung stubbornly to life.

A numbness set in as my fingers were pressed and rolled on the inkpad, their loops and whorls and ridges captured by the fingerprint card. The click of the mugshot camera shutter sealed the deal. *This is for real.*

They made me empty my pockets—wallet, keys, half a roll of Certs, the Olympic token recovered from the side of the gravel road—and deposit the contents into a little box for safekeeping. They even made me surrender my watch.

They led me through the sally port into the tiny cellblock.

The heavy metal bars slammed shut behind me, sequestering me from the outside world. I was alone in a dank, dirty six-by-eight with a rusty World War II vintage metal bunk bed against the far wall, a dirty lidless porcelain toilet in the corner. The wave of dread that had washed over me at the cabin was now a king tide.

I lay on the lower bunk and tried to block out the incessant clamor from the cellblock. I stared at the three metal crossbars and the wire mattress support above me. I traced the rectilinear wire grid, the patterns cast by the light from the dim, flickering ceiling fixture. I imagined an array of yellow three-by-three-inch Post-its clothespinned to the grid, chronicling the events in my life that had led to where I now found myself. I thought about my father, my mother, the brother I didn't know I had, the sister who never was, really. Could the kid on the Schwinn have even conceived that one day he, I, would be lying here in a jail cell?

I was caught in a whirlwind, unable to reconcile the accusations against me. One minute, I was adamant in my denial, convinced of my innocence, and unable to fathom how I could have ended up here. But doubts begin to creep in. A seed of uncertainty took root again. Could I have blacked out and committed an unspeakable act without realizing it? The thought was terrifying, and yet it lingered.

I closed my eyes and saw a spectral John Nash floating across my blood-filled lids like a lost soul grasping for reality on the movie screen. Staring at a wall cluttered with intricate notes and mathematical equations. His eyes filled with rapt concentration and bespeaking inner turmoil, the complex workings of genius and madness intertwined. Struggling to navigate the blurred line between fact and delusion. *A Beautiful Mind* had come out three years ago. I had traveled all the way to Asheville to watch it. To sit in a crowded theater, alone but not alone, and imagine what he must have been going through. Now, as I sat in my assigned cell, I wondered if I was John Nash with a different name. A different story. A different demon.

Barbara had said I could come back when I got my shit together. At the time, I thought I knew what she meant.

I finally managed to drift off to sleep.

* * *

I awoke to the unmistakable blow of a bone-crunching fist raining down hard on my face. I palmed my throbbing cheekbone, ran my fingers across my stubble in search of blood that wasn't there. I frantically scanned the room, but it was empty, save for the relentless clanging metal and constant fuss-kicking echoing off the cold concrete walls from the cell next door. My breath was shallow and fast. I tried to make sense of what had just happened, the lingering sting of the blow putting me on edge. I lay on the thin mattress, the unyielding metal crossbar beneath me cutting into my shoulder blades. I tried hard to reconstruct the minutes, hours, before the blow.

Sometime last night, I had been startled from a deep slumber when I looked up and saw the shadow of a figure gimping toward me. I rose and sat on the bunk's edge. The hulking, blurred-edged and faceless silhouette came closer. I yelled out. *Who are you?* He didn't answer. I rubbed my eyes. Tried to focus. *What do you want?* Still no answer. He towered over me. Then he slipped away.

How long had he stood there in the dark, faceless and mute, before clocking me? Now I lay awake and stared at the mattress support. I held my hand up and traced the wire grid, my index finger cutting a caesura in my line of sight. I followed a circuitous journey across the bed's underbelly, reckoning my own passage. Wondering how and where it would end.

As I lay there, staring at the grid, I noticed a slight movement, a faint jiggle. Had the guards brought in a cellmate in the middle of the night? Had my visitor retreated to the bunk above me after taking liberties with my face? I strained to listen for any sound coming from above.

Then I heard a stirring. A cough. And an unmistakable faint whisper. "Hello, Jack."

I jumped out of bed and checked the upper bunk. There was no one there.

I called out to the guard. My voice echoed against the cellblock walls.

No one came.

With my watch having been taken from me and no clock anywhere, I had no idea what time it was.

Eventually, a guard approached.

"Who entered my cell last night?" I asked.

He looked at me and frowned. He said no one had entered my cell. "Trust me."

"Are you sure?"

"Sure as a heart attack."

"But look." I pointed to my face, my throbbing cheekbone.

"At what?" he said.

I ran over to the sheet of polished metal on the wall above the toilet. Aside from my bloodshot eyes and day-old stubble, my face looked indistinguishable from any other day.

Was it all just a dream?

"When can I get out of here?" I asked.

He said I might be brought before the magistrate as early as this morning. "But don't count on it." He said whenever that did happen, they'd formally charge me, advise me of my rights, and set bail. "Do you have an attorney?" he asked.

"I need one." I thought of the only criminal attorney I knew of in North Carolina. An old codger in Charlotte with a history of getting his clients off. I had read about him in the paper. "I need to make a call."

"Do you have the number?"

"No," I said.

He left, saying he'd return later.

17

PHILIA

I thought back to '98. To the Birmingham abortion clinic bombing that January.

A month later, Eric Rudolph had been fingered as a suspect.

Then a month after that, Daniel Rudolph did his thing with the radial arm saw. Videotaped it. Sent the cassette to the FBI to draw attention to what he perceived as unjust treatment of his brother by the Feds.

I envisioned Daniel walking into his cluttered garage.

> There is a workbench along the wall, with a rotary wall phone at one end. A radial arm saw, with its guard removed, is on the workbench. A tripod is positioned near the bench, with a home movie camera trained on the saw's blade. A King James Bible sits on the bench near the blade. Daniel stands before the bench. He opens the Bible and reads a passage, then closes it and

returns it to the *exact* position where it had been, as if some allegiance to OCD protocol has taken over. He grabs a length of rope and, with his right hand, wraps the ends of the rope several times around his left forearm just below the elbow, crossing them on the outside each time. He ensures the wraps are snug, but not so tight that he can't fit a finger underneath. He takes the two ends of the rope and, with some effort, manages to tie a loose square knot. He grabs a ten-inch Phillips screwdriver from the workbench and inserts it through the knot. He then turns the screwdriver around and around to tighten the tourniquet and, when he deems it sufficiently tight, he wedges the end of the screwdriver between the rope and his arm to keep it in place.

He powers up the saw. The blade roars to life with a metallic hum, blurring into a hypnotic circle, faster than his eye can follow, a silver blur that seems to slice through the air itself. His pulse quickens. His palms grow slick. The room closes in, the machine commanding his full attention Using his right hand, he grabs the saw's handle with a firm grip. He places his left wrist on the saw's platform and pulls the saw toward him. The blade wants to feed itself through flesh. Bone. Sinew. Climbing its way through the cut. Even with the tourniquet in place, blood spatters. On the bench. On the floor. On his work shirt. On the Bible. He grabs a towel and rushes to the phone. He removes the receiver and cradles it between his shoulder and ear. His right hand trembles as he places his finger in the 9 hole, rotates the dial to the finger stop, and releases it. Then 1. Then 1 again. He waits, hoping against hope that his consciousness will hold until help arrives.

Everything happened so quickly. The press was reporting it within a day. When had Daniel sent the cassette off to the authorities? Did he expect the FBI to share the details with the media so soon? Was that his intent all along? I wondered.

My mind then shifted to an unnamed family's living room in a split-level on a cul-de-sac in a tree-lined neighborhood somewhere. Anywhere, really.

> Mother, father, and kids are gathered around the Magnavox waiting for the news to wrap up before "The Wonderful World of Disney" starts at seven. The mother and father are sitting on the divan. The kids are cross-legged on the floor. All eyes are glued to the screen. A reporter comes on. "Yesterday, March 7th, Birmingham bombing suspect Eric Rudolph's brother Daniel videotaped himself cutting off his left hand with a radial arm saw in order to, in his words, send a message to the FBI and the media. Doctors believe they will be able to successfully reattach his hand."

What must my imaginary family have thought? How did the kids react? How did the parents react? Did the father rush over to the TV and change the channel. What did the parents say to their children? How did they explain such a horrific act?

18

Release

The following morning, I was finally brought before the magistrate, who was housed in the section of the building where the sheriff was.

He was in a suit and tie and sitting behind a small desk. In a nondescript room, dimly lit and devoid of any semblance of personality. The desk was sturdy but crude, its surface marred by what I assumed was years of ink stains and scratches. The rollers on the chair where he sat let out a soft squeak whenever he shifted his considerable weight.

Never having been in a situation like this before, I had envisioned a courtroom like you would see on TV. And a robed judge sitting behind a judicial bench. But we *were* in a small town, after all, and I had no reason to believe, *Perry Mason* notwithstanding, that what I was seeing was anything but typical.

I stood across the desk from the magistrate.

He asked if I had an attorney.

I said no, but I would soon.

He asked about the whys and wherefores of my situation. Not the crimes I had been accused of, but my personal comings and goings. My background. Where I lived. Where I worked, which was nowhere, I told him.

He leaned forward, hands clasped, and recited the charges against me—arson, second-degree murder with a possibility of reduction to manslaughter. My rights—to remain silent, to be represented by an attorney. Next steps—Superior Court, arraignment, trial.

"It is customary to deny bail," he said, "until a bond hearing can be held before a Superior Court judge. However, I do have some discretion in these matters. Taking into consideration the mitigating factors, I've decided to exercise that discretion and set bail at $75,000. You will be required to meet this amount to secure release pending further proceedings."

And that was that. No elaboration of mitigating factors. No opportunity to profess my innocence. No discussion of how bail was set. But one thing was crystal clear. Unless I coughed up the clams, I would remain behind bars. However long it took, until the slow wheels of justice finally brought about a trial.

Later that morning, I got to make the call I had been anticipating. I phoned the Charlotte attorney I'd read about in the paper. He arranged for an associate to meet me at the jail tomorrow afternoon, the twenty-eighth.

I returned to my cell with plenty of time on my hands to try to figure out what to do next.

Around 3:30, a guard appeared. "C'mon," he said. "You're outta here."

"What do you mean, I'm outta here?"

"Your bail's been made."

I stood, nonplussed, in the middle of my cell. "Who would have done that?"

"Above my pay grade," the guard said.

I was escorted to the discharge area. I signed a stack of papers, including a promise to adhere to strict travel restrictions while out on bail and to appear in court when ordered to do so.

"Left or right?" the jailer asked.

"Excuse me?"

He held the ankle monitor in front of me. "Left or right?"

"Left," I said.

He locked the monitor in place then ushered me to my next destination, where a fastidious woman in a crisp guard uniform reviewed the inventory of personal belongings that had been taken from me. I signed a receipt acknowledging the return of everything.

I was about to walk out of the jail a free man, albeit temporarily and having no idea how I would get back to my cabin, when I was approached by another prison official.

"Your taxi is waiting outside."

"My taxi?" I replied. "You guys provide taxi service now?"

"No," he said with an under-the-breath chuckle. "We don't do that. Your bail maker sent it."

I asked who my "bail maker" was. He thumbed through his paperwork. "Says here they've asked to remain anonymous."

On the way home, I asked the taxi driver if he knew who had arranged and paid for my ride.

"No idea," he said. "I got the call. I took it. That's all she wrote."

I racked my brain trying to think of who my benefactor could be? Who could have known of my plight? Of my arrest two days prior? Of the setting of my bail? Could my father have somehow found out? But how?

About halfway between Murphy and my cabin, I remembered that I was supposed to meet with the attorney at the jail tomorrow afternoon. But I obviously wouldn't be there. *I'll call first thing in the morning and let him know I'm out but will get to Charlotte as soon as I can.*

I sat in the quiet of my cabin. The monitor's strap dug deep into my skin. The module itself hugged my ankle, a constant reminder that I was anything but a free man. That I was being tracked wherever I went. And *wherever I went* had taken on new meaning. My comings and goings had been restricted to Murphy, a narrow corridor along Highway 19 between Murphy and my cabin, and the town of Marble—the latter a concession, no doubt, so I could continue my periodic Big D runs. *Thank you, judge, for your thoughtfulness.*

I was torn. On the one hand, I needed to meet with my attorney as soon as possible to deal with the charges that had been leveled against me. But on the other hand, ever since discovering the photo and birth certificate in my childhood closet, and learning from my father of David Pate's pedigree, I yearned to find out more. To seek out the spore of my split-branch sibling. His absentee father, until *I* came along and the little bastard—as my own father surely called him—was whisked away to live with that other family.

I would have to return to Georgia. To cross the divide between *free in a sense* and *near-certain relapse into captivity*?

I would sleep on it. Maybe by morning I'd have come to my senses and accepted that nothing is worth risking a return to the slammer.

* * *

I bolted military straight from a sound sleep. I rubbed my eyes with my knuckles and waited for the blear to dissolve. The clock said ten 'til three. Somehow, in the depths of slumber, my hippocampus had tracked down a long-suppressed memory and forced it out. A recollection of a little boy half-hiding under his bed. Of a carving in the bed rail's hard maple. Of three baseball cards secured with a stiff and fragile pink rubber band. Of the initials in blue ink on the back.

1978

19

DP

Whenever Daddy said I was cruisin' for a bruisin', I knew he meant it.

It usually started with Mama yelling, "Earnest, bring your strap." Daddy almost never started the whole thing, but he was always the one to finish it. Mama never laid a hand on me. Whatever *she* did, she did with words. Daddy would come running—stumbling's more like it—into my bedroom, with a crazy twisted-up face and with the belt in his hand.

This afternoon was different, though. This time, when he swung open my bedroom door and stormed into my room, he didn't have the belt. He was holding one of those leather things barbers use to sharpen their razors. A *real* strap. It was a lot wider and thicker than a belt, and there was a metal hook on one end. But he had that same scary look he always had when he paid a visit to my room.

It had all started a few hours earlier. I had come home from school with a note from my teacher Miss Strickland. The note was sealed in an envelope, so I didn't know what it said.

Mama made me stand before her while she opened it and read it out loud. "Mrs. Pate," it said, "please arrange to come to the school for a conference with Mr. Tidwell and me." Mama looked up from the note with a scowl. Then she continued. "For the past week, Jack has insisted that his imaginary friend sit beside him in class. He gets agitated and talks incessantly. He won't pay attention. It's very disruptive and annoying to his classmates. Then he goes from keyed up to crying, which causes even more disruption. I've consulted with Mr. Tidwell, and we believe counseling may be in order." Mama folded the note and returned it to its envelope. "So what is this about, Jack?"

I puffed out my chest with an attitude. "It's nothin' Mama. That Miss Strickland, she's just an old wrinkled-up bitch." As soon as that last word slipped out, I knew I was a goner.

"Just wait 'til your father gets home," Mama said.

I retreated to my room to wait for what was to come. I sat on the bed, my legs dangling off the edge like lifeless strangers trying to find their owner. I sometimes wondered what it would be like to lose control of my limbs, nothing but numbness. Then I wouldn't feel the stings from Daddy's belt.

After the belting, after Daddy had stormed out of my bedroom just as fast as he'd stormed in, after Mama's *Good Jack, Bad Jack* thing, I retreated to my little closet hidey-hole. I sat on the floor fighting back the tears. I ran my hand down my thigh, redder and more swollen than usual because of that thick, hard strap.

Mama and Daddy couldn't understand why I was the way I was. Nobody understood except my best friends. The ones that are there when nobody else wants to be, the ones only I can see. They make me feel good when other people don't. My friends know I'm a good boy. They know I'm not Bad Jack.

But in my hidey-hole, as I forced down the lump in my throat, my friends weren't with me. I called out, but nobody came.

I looked around for something to help me get my mind off things.

My eyes fell on the shoebox with my Braves cards. I sat with it in my lap and removed the lid. There was Gary Matthews. Phil Niekro. Biff Pocoroba—I always had a hard time saying his last name right, and I thought his first name was just plain silly.

At the bottom of the stack there were these three cards wrapped in a rubber band that was so old it had stopped snapping a long time ago. I removed the rubber band, careful not to break it, just like always. There was Filipe Alou. And Joe Torre. And Tony Cloninger. The cards all said '67. I wasn't even born then. I'd always wondered where these cards came from and how they ended up in my box. The other curious thing was that all three of 'em had DP written on the back in blue ink. I would never ask Mama and Daddy about the cards and who they belonged to. I'd learned a long time ago not to ask questions about anything like that. Especially after a licking. Best to keep my mouth shut. But the bigger reason I didn't ask was because one time when I was lying under my bed, pretending to be hiding from the Viet Cong, I saw those same initials—DP—carved into the bottom bed rail. I was scared to say anything because Mama and Daddy might accuse *me* of being the one that did the carving.

2004

20

WACO

Accepting the inevitable, that there was no way I'd be able to go back to sleep, I staggered into the kitchen.

Cajmere—Gino Vittori, Green Velvet—wormed his way into my ear. I have no idea why. I hate techno four-on-the-floor house music. *It's time for the perculator. It's time for the perculator.* What would Yardley Bennett have thought? *Dance floor drivel posing as music. And the man can't even pronounce percolator correctly. What plebeian nonsense. Montovani's surely turning in his grave.* I chuckled, but with a dose of riled resolve thrown in. My nowhere-to-be-found darkling drifter had a way with words, that's for sure. But I feared his own actions just may have contributed to my current plight. I still needed to track him down, but I seemed to have exhausted my efforts, at least for the time being.

For now, I had more pressing issues to deal with. A passel of legal troubles. And a long-lost half-brother I didn't know I had.

I brewed a pot in the *perculator*, poured myself a cup, and sat at the table pondering what daybreak would bring. Any hope I may have had of coming to my senses and accepting that nothing is worth risking a return to the slammer had been dashed. I had already split town once when told not to and gotten away with it. When the deputy sheriff had said stay nearby, and I took off to Villa Rica anyway. But this time, the warning was a bit more official, being that it came straight from the judge. And now I was being tracked electronically. But I'd take my chances. Somebody once said live life every day on the edge because you never know when that edge might be gone. I'd get the job done as quickly as I could, then I'd head straight to Charlotte.

I had chosen to try to identify David Michael Pate's father rather than find David himself. I rationalized this by telling myself that, surely, David would have been reassigned his father's surname. And without a name to run with, I had no chance of finding him. Maybe that was why I sought the father first. Or maybe it was because I feared encountering my half-brother face-to-face. What would I say to him? Would we have anything in common? Or would the encounter dredge up even more repressed childhood memories? For me and for him.

Halfway to Atlanta, as soon as I knew the Charlotte attorney's office would be open, I stopped at a pay phone and dialed him. I told him I'd been released, but I had no idea who had posted bail. "How is that possible?"

"It's not common," he said. "But it does happen sometimes."

I asked him if he could find out who did it.

"When bail is posted," he said, "the courts typically don't require the person paying the bail or the jurisdiction receiving the bail to inform defense of his identity. This payment can be made directly to the court or through a bondsman, and the bail payer can remain anonymous to both the defense attorney and the defendant. The only identification required is proof of payment or a bail bond receipt."

"Do you mean I may never find out?"

"That's correct. We may not be informed of the person's identity unless this information becomes relevant to the case. That said, there's still a chance you may learn who it is at some point."

I told my attorney I had to take care of something first—I didn't tell him I was leaving the state—but that I hoped to come see him within a couple of days. He said okay, but I should meet with him as soon as possible to sign the engagement letter, pay him his retainer, and "get down to business."

I hung up frustrated but resigned that my benefactor, at least in the short term, would remain anonymous.

For now, I would focus on my immediate task at hand and soldier on to Atlanta.

When I got to the city, I parked in the surface lot across Linden Avenue from Crawford Long Hospital. I marveled at the building's grandeur, with its massive ionic columns and neoclassical portico. Any change in the building's façade since my last visit to the hospital, in the summer of '76 for a tonsillectomy, was lost on me.

The receptionist directed me down the hall.

A woman was sitting at a single-pedestal steel desk just inside the door to the Administrative Offices.

I asked where I might find a physician directory from '63 or thereabouts. "There's some urgency to my request," I said, knowing

I was on thin ice, a hundred miles from my confinement area and needing to get back before I was found out.

She said just a minute and crossed the room. I saw her conferring with a man in a half-partition office, the kind with fluted glass running from waist-high to the partition's top. He walked over to his office doorway, looked across the room at me, then returned his attention to the woman.

She came back over to where I was standing. "You'll need to go to Emory across town. That's where they keep the archives." She took a notepad from her desk drawer and wrote something on it. She tore off the top sheet and handed it to me. "Five forty Asbury Circle. Ask for Mildred. She can provide you with what you need. I'll call ahead and tell her you're on your way." She smiled. "May I tell her you're on your way?"

I said yes. I thanked her and made straight to the Land Rover.

Mildred had me sit at a table in a small room off to the side of the main room. She brought three volumes and set them down before me. "These aren't just the doctors. They're all the staff, the nurses, the board, everybody. And it's all the hospitals, too. The main one across campus. Plus Emory Clinic, Crawford Long, Wesley Woods. The whole shebang. It's divided up by hospital, though. I couldn't find '63. But here's '60, '65, and '70."

"These'll do just fine, ma'am."

I had brought with me the photograph of the dapper man in sport coat and fedora that I had discovered in my childhood closet.

I opened '65 and turned to the listing of physicians. But I realized Mildred was still standing over me. I looked up and raised my eyebrows.

"Oh. I'll leave you be," she said, and scurried away.

There were a hundred or so doctors listed for Crawford Long. These included attending physicians, residents, specialists. As I thumbed through the pages, it occurred to me that I had no idea what I was doing. It felt like—what did Yogi Berra call it?—déjà vu all over again. I had gone through the same damned wild-goose exercise in my phone book search for Yardley Bennett. Only then, I had a presumed name to go on. This time, I had nothing. No name. No description. No specific medical field like neurology or pediatrics or gynecology. And, except for the medical director and department heads, there were no accompanying pictures.

The directory had an alphabetical section in the front. Behind that was a section organized by hospital and area of specialization. It also noted where each physician went to medical school, when they graduated, when they went into practice, and any special designations, like FACS or FACP.

My father had said the man was a specialist, but he claimed not to know more than that. I skipped over the sections of general physicians, hospitalists, residents, interns.

Knowing my mother as I did, or should I say had, I assumed she would have gone after somebody roughly my father's age. But I didn't see how that was possible. If my father had attended medical school, which would have been about as likely as my joining the Metropolitan Opera, he would have graduated around '61. Was it reasonable to assume that someone graduating around that time already would have been a practicing specialist when David was born? Not likely. That told me the man must have been older. But not too much older, assuming my mother would have exercised some age-gap reluctance. I decided to eliminate anyone who had graduated before '51 or after '60. That alone, and eliminating nonspecialists, allowed me to narrow the field down a lot, to no more than thirty-five or so names. I whipped out my notepad and began jotting them down. When I got almost to the end of the Radiology section, my breath held captive for a moment.

DAVID KELLNER YARDLEY M.D.   MEDICAL
COLLEGE OF GEORGIA 1953   RADIOLOGIST 1959

David Yardley? David Pate? Yardley Bennett?

I sought out Mildred. "Can you look up a Crawford Long physician for me?" I gave her David Kellner Yardley's name.

She came back a few minutes later. "I'm sorry, Mr. Pate. Unfortunately, Dr. Yardley passed away five years ago."

"Do you have an obituary?"

"We would have one on file, but it will take me a while to retrieve it." She looked at her watch. "And it's lunchtime. Could you perhaps come back in an hour? Actually, give me an hour and a half. I'll have it for you when you return."

I left the building and walked over to Emory Village. I ducked into the Falafel King. I bought a lamb gyro and a soft drink.

I was halfway through my lunch when I became aware that someone was standing over me. I looked up.

It was Yardley Bennett. "What are you doing here?" he said.

On the one hand, I was glad he had resurfaced. On the other hand, I was baffled, yet again, that he somehow knew where to find me. "What are *you* doing here?"

"If I told you I was slumming, you probably wouldn't believe me."

"Does the name David Yardley mean anything to you?"

"I like the name. Especially the last name."

"That's not what I asked."

"No, it means nothing to me."

I looked around the room. Every eye was trained on me. "Listen, I don't know why you're following me," I said. "I don't know what you want. But this is not the time or place to confront whatever your issues are, whatever fucking obsession you're pursuing. My life's been nothing but a living hell since you first graced my door. I have my own immediate issues to contend with. If you want to know the truth, I—"

"If *I* were on the lam from the law, I wouldn't be quite so impertinent."

"On the lam? What do you mean, on the lam?"

"Well, let's just say you're treading on dangerous ground right now."

"What would *you* know?"

He sat down across the table from me and leaned in. "What I know is that I've gone out of my way to try to help you. But you don't seem to get it. The black dog, Jack Pate. Muzzle it." He stood and began walking away. As he was walking out the door, he turned around. "I'm leaving now. You're on your own."

Not wanting him to slip through my fingers again, I jumped up and ran after him. "I'm sorry, Yardley," I yelled. "I don't want you to go. It's just that I have a lot of shit going on right now. Come back, please, and let's talk some more."

He was already halfway down the block when he turned around to face me. "We'll reconvene in time, my friend. In time." Then he ducked into a narrow alleyway.

I ran to the alley. But he had disappeared.

I returned to the restaurant, gathered my things, and left. Confused and dispirited.

When I got back to Mildred's desk, she handed me a photocopy of the obituary.

Dr. David Kellner Yardley, dedicated physician, beloved husband and father, passed away peacefully on May 5th at the age of 71. Born in 1928, Dr. Yardley devoted his life to the practice of medicine and the care of his patients.

Dr. Yardley graduated from the Medical College of Georgia in 1953, embarking on a career marked by compassion, skill, and an unwavering commitment to his patients' well-being. Throughout his decades-long career, he touched countless lives, providing expert medical care and a kind and listening ear.

A lifelong resident of Waco, Georgia, he is survived by his loving wife, Janice (née Bennett), and son, David, who were his greatest sources of pride and joy. He is preceded in death by his father, Dr. Francis

Kellner Yardley, and his mother, Emmaline Bray Yardley.

Dr. Yardley was known for his gentle spirit, warmth, and the deep love he held for his family, friends, and the community he cared for so deeply.

A private service will be held for family and close friends. In lieu of flowers, the family kindly requests that donations be made to The American Cancer Society.

Née Bennett? Waco?

Accompanying the obit was a headshot.

I retrieved the photograph I had brought with me and compared the two. Accounting for what I imagined thirty years of aging would have begotten, the men in the pictures looked similar.

I thanked Mildred and hurried back to my Land Rover. It would take me two hours max to get to Waco.

I rolled into Waco proper and stopped at the first gas station I saw. I asked the attendant if he had a phone book. "White or yellow," he said.

"White."

I flipped through to the Ys. Ran my finger down the short list until I came to Janice Yardley. I asked for directions to the address shown.

The attendant said, "Go back to the 27 Bypass. Hang a right. About halfway to Carrollton, you'll see a sign on the righthand side of the highway that says turn to go to Gray Field…that's our airport, if you can call it that…don't turn there, though. A little past that sign, you'll see a road to the right with a big ol' iron gate. Take it. Chances are the gate'll be open. I haven't seen it closed since ol' man Yardley crossed over. You can't miss it."

"So, you knew him?"

"Everybody knew the doctor. Fine man. Did a lot for people in these parts."

"Do you know his son?"

"Nobody ever sees him. I suppose he moved away a long time ago and doesn't come back much, if at all."

Contrary to what the attendant had predicted, the gate to the Yardley residence was closed. As "big ol'" gates go, this was one of the biggest I'd seen. Ornate wrought iron embellished with fancy ornamentation and topped by a D on the left half and a Y on the right. The wrought iron was flanked by two ten-foot-high brick-and-stone posts with large concrete pineapple finials. But the condition of the gate, with its rusted verticals, its broken hinges, belied its past grandeur.

I got out of the Land Rover and eased the left half of the gate open, careful not to cause it to collapse before me.

The pea gravel road from the gate to the house was long, winding, and rutted.

The desolate and forlorn house, surrounded by wild tangles of weeds and half-dead oaks whose branches stretched like gnarled fingers toward the sky, loomed before me. Its once-grand Federal-style columns were now chipped and leaning as if struggling to support the roofline. Shuttered windows, veiled in grime, stared blankly. The paint hung like loose skin on the cracked trim.

A wave of apprehension rose through my chest and lodged in my throat.

I wondered whether anyone was at home, as there were no vehicles in the forecourt and it was dead quiet all around me.

I parked and climbed the steps to the front door. I lifted the knocker and released it. The resonating clang broke the silence.

The door eased open.

But there was no one there.

I called out. There was no reply.

I gingerly crossed the threshold into an unlit foyer.

I called out again.

Straight ahead was a winding staircase. To my right and left were massive pocket doors. The one on my right was closed. The other one was partially open. Enough for me to pass through, which I did.

I found myself standing in what appeared to be a parlor. But the drapes were closed and the lights were off, preventing me from making out much.

As I stood there in the dark room, a chill swept over me. I sensed I was not alone.

I was about to turn around, head to my Land Rover, and retrieve my Stoeger from the wayback when the voice called out. "I've been waiting for you."

1978

21

FIXATION

hildhood neurosis. I'd never heard that second word, and I wasn't sure what it meant.

The doctor was wearing a bow tie and leather suspenders, which I thought was funny for a minute. But then I realized there wasn't anything funny about where we were.

"Has he experienced trauma that you're aware of?" he asked Mama, never looking at me, as if I wasn't even there. He could have looked me in the eye if he had wanted to, because Mama and I were sitting next to each other on the couch, and he was in a chair right across from us.

"Why, of course not," Mama replied. She looked down at me. "How could little Jack have had trauma at *his* age?"

I tried hard to hold Bad Jack back, to keep him from bursting out.

I could just hear what Daddy would say if he'd been here. *Trauma? Nothin' a good whuppin' won't cure. These kids these days, I swear, they don't have any idea about hardship. Trauma my ass. Let me tell you what it was like when I was his age.* I knew he would have said it because I'd heard it before. Not the trauma part but the other stuff.

The doctor went on. Most of the time, I wouldn't have paid a lot of attention to somebody who didn't even look at me. But this time, I focused on every word, even if I didn't understand half of it. I had to. I felt like my whole future was on the line.

"Imaginary companions," he said, "especially at his late age, coupled with disruptive behavior and bouts of crying can sometimes be indicators of an underlying response to trauma or depression, or both, though these behaviors are not definitive signs on their own."

Now *I* was the one that refused to look at *him*. Anybody that would disrespect my friends and try to blame it on depression didn't deserve to know I was paying him any attention.

He tossed out questions like a machine gun. "How's his appetite? What are his sleeping habits? Does he have attention problems? How are his grades?"

Jeez, I thought. *This guy sure is nosy.*

Mama rattled off the answers like she knew the questions ahead of time and had rehearsed the whole thing. "Okay for a growing boy. Not very good, he sometimes has bad dreams. Hard time concentrating unless it's things he's fixated on, like fires and explosions. As and Bs mainly."

"Tell me about the fixation on fires and explosions."

Here we go, I thought.

Mama said it was probably because my daddy's a fireman.

After he'd asked a bunch more questions, the doctor got up and walked over to his desk. He grabbed a little notepad and a pen and sat back down. He scribbled something on the pad. Then he ripped it off and gave it to Mama. "I'm prescribing something called a TCA. A tricyclic antidepressant. But you don't need to worry about the details. Let's try it and see if things improve. It's a very low dose." He pulled his glasses down on his nose and looked at Mama over the rims. "But use it with care. And only as directed. It can have side effects. And there's an overdose risk."

He rose from his chair. "See me back here in two weeks. Miss Abernathy can schedule an appointment."

As we were about to walk out, he finally paid attention to me. He looked at me and said, "Good luck, son. I hope things get better for you."

On the way home, Mama didn't say a word. I didn't either. That is until, about halfway to our house, it just somehow came out of my mouth, like *bitch* had the other day. "Mama, who's DP?" I was sure Bad Jack had blurted it. There's no way Good Jack would have had the nerve to say something like that. Or *bitch*.

Mama swerved and almost ran over the curb and onto the sidewalk. She stopped the car and put it in Park. She turned to me and, for the first time ever, I thought her head might explode. She was red and shaking something awful. "Where did you hear that?"

"I didn't hear it," I said. "I saw it with these things here, with my own two eyes. On my baseball cards and carved into my bed."

"Jack," she said. "There are some things that aren't meant for little boys to know or talk about. You're not to bring it up again. Not with me. And *certainly* not with your father."

I never brought it up again.

2004

22

GENEROSITY

cross the parlor was a tri-panel folding screen. I couldn't tell much in the dark, but it looked like it had trees and birds and Chinese characters on it.

A figure emerged from behind the screen and approached me. "Is this where the journey ends?" As he neared, features materialized. "I had hoped things would end differently, Jack Pate."

"Did you?"

"For years."

"You're not Yardley Bennett, are you? You're David."

"You got me there. Finally, maybe some of those blank pages you talked about so disparagingly are beginning to fill with particulars. What some might call details and *shit*. Right?" He grinned.

"Why, David? Why did you seek me out? What do you want from me?"

"What I want from you, my brother…may I call you brother?… is something you can't give me. I learned that the hard way."

"And that is?"

He walked across the room and drew open the drapes. The outside light delineated his gaunt figure, bringing back the memory of the first time I had laid eyes on him.

In the light of the late afternoon sun, I realized we were in a library.

He took a seat in the wingback chair beside the window and motioned for me to sit in the matching one across from him. "I told you once that I'm a stickler for the rubric and refused to let you skim through the pages to get to the good part. Well, Jack Pate, you've earned the right, I suppose, to know more."

"That would help. Because, right now, I must admit, I'm stupefied."

"I cared about you," he said. "But I also resented you. I resented everything you had that I *never* had. Never hoped to have, I suppose. And the thing is, you let it all slip away. You were so thick. Surprising, given your pedagogical upbringing. Anyway, I thought maybe I could help you. But then again, why would I want to help the person I resented so much?"

"I'm sorry, David. I really am."

"The last thing I need is pity." He stood, reached down, and placed his hand on my shoulder. "Nor do you. Pity accomplishes nothing. Compassion, on the other hand—"

I drew back. "And resentment?"

He straightened back up. "Care for a drink? I make a killer rye Manhattan. And my father insisted on top-shelf. Does Van Winkle Reserve suit your taste?"

I nodded. Hard liquor was not my thing, but given the current circumstances, I would down it with zeal.

He returned with the drinks and sat back down.

I took a swallow. The whiskey greeted my palate with a smooth warmth, not the fiery punch I had expected. It blossomed in my chest. For a fleeting moment, I was somewhere else. I wanted to savor the experience, one of life's little diversions from reality, a bit longer.

But he continued. "Maybe you should know a little more about me. About what I've been through. I've had money, goddamn I've had plenty of it. And access to a good education…if I chose to avail myself of it. My father saw to that.

"But none of that means a whit in the grand scheme. When I was almost six, and my mother…my *real* mother…sent me away, I lost everything that mattered most. You? You were her golden boy. And me? I was the one she wanted to wipe out of her mind. The bitter fruit of her bitter offense. Not quite Hester-Prynne-worthy, but close enough.

"Sure, she visited from time to time at Barkley Hall, the military academy my father and that other one, Janice, sent me off to, but it was clear I was the outcast. Then she stopped coming. What was I? Sixteen? That's when I made it my life's mission to seek you out. To dog you to the bitter end." He walked across the room and took a book from the shelf. "Have you read Freud?" He held up his palm. "You don't need to answer that, I already suspect you have. Well, I became the Thanatos to your Eros."

"But," I protested, "you make it sound like I had an idyllic childhood, David. It wasn't that way at all. Okay, they cared for me, I know they did, but I can't say they were loving parents most of the time. Especially my crapulent father. When he was on the bottle, he would—"

David held up his palm again. "Stop. I don't care what they did or didn't do to you, Jack. They gave you one thing I never had."

"What's that?" I asked.

"Attention, Jack. They gave you attention. They were generous to you in a way you've never seemed to appreciate."

"If that's what they were giving me…generosity…it sure didn't feel that way at the time."

He asked me if I had ever heard of a French philosopher named Simone Weil.

I said I had heard the name, but that was about it.

He sat back down across from me. "She once spoke words that I want you never, ever, to forget, okay?"

"Okay."

"She said attention is the rarest and purest form of generosity. That's love, Jack Pate. Pure and simple."

"Love? You could have fooled me."

"Maybe they did the best they could. Maybe they didn't know better. Maybe they thought they were doing the right thing. I sometimes think about the fact that we humans have been rearing children for millennia. You would think we would have gotten it right by now. But we may be no smarter today than we were two thousand years ago."

He reminded me that he had once asked whether I really knew my own children.

Now, I knew what to say, but I couldn't get the words out.

"You could have been somebody," he continued. "Hell, you *were* somebody. You had a loving wife, two adorable children, a successful career. All the things I didn't have. And then you blew it. You let the black dog destroy it all. Not just for you, but for those around you."

"How long have you been following me?" I asked.

"*Following* you? If that's the word you choose, I guess I'll accept it."

"What word would *you* choose?"

He stood back up. Paced the room a couple of times. Then returned to his chair. "How about *shadowed*? Do you like that word? Ever since I turned nineteen. You were…let's see…a mere lad of fourteen as I recall."

"Since I was fourteen? Are you kidding me?"

He grinned. "Jack Pate, I think you're improving."

"What do you mean?"

"You didn't say *shitting* me this time. Right?"

"I guess not."

"Hell, I wanted to *be* you. But I knew I couldn't. I decided the next best thing would be to try to show you the errors of your ways, to help you recover what you'd lost. But you didn't seem to want that. At least that's the way *I* saw it."

"Why didn't you just level with me from the beginning?"

He lit a cigarette. Blew smoke rings. "Oh, I couldn't do that, Jack Pate. Where would the adventure have been? The intrigue? The subterfuge? If life's not a game, it's not worth living."

"So, half what you told me isn't true. Your name, for example."

"It worked. *You* fell for it, didn't you?"

"The car dealership? Wife and kids? Five Forks Forty-niner? Wabash College?"

"I really did go to Wabash, for three semesters. Then I dropped out. As for the other things, what did I once tell you?"

"You told me a lot of things."

"I said if I set out to tell you the truth, I'd have to lie. It's in my nature."

"You did say that. Fair warning, I guess."

"But some things I said were true. Dead-on true. Like the time, when we first met, when I said, implied anyway, that you don't know your children. If I'm not mistaken, you agreed with me then. Sort of. I just brought it up again, and your silence speaks volumes. You *do* agree with me, don't you?"

I nodded. Tears welled.

"Attention, Jack," he said. "Attention is love." He walked over and placed his hand on my shoulder again. "Do me a favor, Jack. Get the help you need. The help you've needed for years and refused to acknowledge. And go back to your family. I think it's time."

I looked up at him. "I'm in trouble, David. More trouble than you could possibly imagine."

"I know about the trouble you're in." He lit another cigarette. "Take a chance. Go back to Villa Rica, Jack."

"But what about the authorities?" I held out my leg. Pointed to the ankle bracelet. "What about this?"

"Go, Jack. Live on the edge. Go back now. It'll all work out."

I asked him what his plans were, what would happen to him.

"Don't worry about me," he said. "I always wanted to be somebody, just like you were somebody before you lost it all. I *am* somebody now. It took you to help me, but I now have a legacy that will live on after I'm gone."

"What do you mean?"

He excused himself and retreated behind the folding screen and into the adjacent room.

I waited for him to return. I called out his name, but he didn't answer.

After twenty minutes that felt like an hour, I decided to go looking for him. I searched every room in the house, but he wasn't there.

From the upstairs bedroom window, I noticed a two-car garage in the back.

23

LEGACY

I was about to step away from the window when I saw one of the garage doors open. A Land Rover, identical to mine except for the dent on the right front quarter panel, went speeding out of the garage, past the far side of the house and toward the street. I bounded down the stairs, but by the time I reached the front yard, it was already halfway down the driveway, pea gravel flying in every direction in its wake. There was no way I'd be able to catch up with it.

The last thing David Pate, aka Yardley Bennett, had said to me outside the Falafel King before he disappeared into the alleyway was *In time, my friend. In time.* Now I understood.

I ran through the house and into the back yard. I entered the garage through the open door. A wall separated where the Land Rover had been from the other half of the garage. There was a standard-sized door with a deadbolt lock at the far end of the wall.

I tried the knob, but the door was locked. I clenched my jaw, took a step back, and rammed my heel hard onto where the locking mechanism met the doorframe. The impact came with a resounding thud, followed instantly by a sharp crack. The wood gave way, splintering into jagged shards that burst outward like a shattered wave.

The other half of the garage was a workshop. But it wasn't just any workshop. My eyes fell first on the wooden workbench stretching across the wall. There was a radial arm saw on the bench. And a Bible. A tripoded movie camera stood trained on the saw blade.

Had I just unknowingly spent the past month, off and on, with Daniel Rudolph? Or was this just another of David Michael Pate's deceptions?

Once I was able to pry my eyes away from the bench, I looked around the room. The wall behind me was cluttered, floor-to-ceiling, with scribbled notes, photographs, newspaper articles.

I was immediately reminded of the wall in the shack behind John Nash's house.

Only in this case, most of the items related to Eric Rudolph and his brother Daniel. The Olympic Park and abortion clinic bombings. The gay nightclub bombing. The manhunt. Daniel's hand-severing protest. Eric's arrest behind the convenience store.

But interspersed among these items, there were also articles about the Tomotla fire. The other fires in the vicinity of Marble. Stanley Jacobs' death. The Fulton Industrial bombing.

I happened to notice a 2004 wall calendar, turned to January, hanging on the front wall of the room. To the left of the 1/1 square, a 12/31 square had been penned in. Handwritten inside that square was the word TOMOTLA.

Inside the 1/3 square, JACK PATE.

I quickly scanned down the month, past the handwritten annotations for the other North Carolina fires and the Fulton Industrial bombing, to today. Inside 1/28, one word. GOODBYE.

I was about to run back inside the house to call the authorities when my eyes fell on the Bible. There was a piece of paper sticking out, about a quarter of the way into the book. I opened to the page.

The paper was a $75,000 bail bond receipt from the Cherokee County magistrate.

Stunned, I read the marked passage.

2 Samuel 14:30.

Then he said to his servants, "Look, Joab's field is next to mine, and he has barley there. Go and set it on fire." So Absalom's servants set the field on fire.

The underline was penned in bright red.

What had David told me as we stood in the parlor? *I now have a legacy that will live on after I'm gone.*

24

LIVE IT

Late Friday morning. The 30th of January.
I sat across from my attorney.

I had spent Wednesday, what was left of it, and Thursday dealing with the Haralson County, Georgia authorities and revisiting my dad before bypassing my cabin and heading straight to Charlotte. I had refrained from telling my dad about David. I just couldn't bring myself to. Not yet.

"All charges against you have been dropped," my attorney said. "David Pate turned himself in to the Cherokee County sheriff yesterday."

I was shocked but relieved. My attorney said David had confessed to the North Carolina fires, to causing Stanley Jacobs' death, although he denied intending to kill the man. Remembering the newspaper's reference to Jacobs somehow being incapacitated to prevent him from escaping, I questioned David's claim. But I kept that to myself. Whatever the facts, he and the courts would have to deal with it, and I undoubtedly would be called. A time and place for everything.

I extended my leg. "I guess I need to get my shackle removed."

My attorney instructed me to return to the sheriff's office. He said they would take care of that right away. He had me sign a bunch of papers and said I was good to go.

"How much do I owe you?" I asked.

"You're settled up."

"What do you mean, I'm settled up?"

"It's all taken care of."

"By whom?"

"David Pate."

If I headed straight to Murphy, I could get to the sheriff's office before five.

On the drive over, I replayed the events of the past month.

I thought about the stranger who had showed up at my door in the dead of night. The stranger I now knew as my half-brother. How he had entered my life for real after *shadowing* me—his word—for two decades. How he had tried to help me see the light in his own twisted way. How he had posted my bail, paid my attorney, his last acts of apparent generosity.

When the time came, I would indeed end up having to testify against him, an ordeal I anticipated with a heavy dose of unease.

I thought about my dad. And my mom, rest her soul. Somehow, in the moment, magnanimity consumed me. David was right. My parents had done the best they could, given their own limitations.

I thought about Barbara and the kids.

I thought about the black dog.

Halfway to Murphy, a wave of tearful melancholia hit me hard. I had to pull over and give it time to pass.

"Can't remove it," the deputy said.

"What do you mean, you can't remove it?"

"The jail put it on. The jail'll have to take it off. That's just the way it is." He pointed down the hallway. "Jail's rahtchere. But you knew that already."

The dread I had felt the last time I had entered the jail was gone. But in the quiet corners of my mind, where shadows linger longer than light, I felt a numbness. Not the paralyzing grip of dread, but rather a gentle, downcast weight. A regret that things had turned out the way they had. A grieving for what could have been.

After the ankle monitor had been removed, I requested to see David.

"Are you a relative?" the jail clerk asked.

My throat seized up. I barely got out Yes.

"Let me check." The clerk left.

A few minutes later she returned. "He'll see you." A guard ushered me to the visitation room.

I thought back again to our first meeting. His hollow eyes morphing to mysterious black holes. His cut-glass gaze turning to blue tourmaline. His million dollar smile and sparkling number 5. His *top of the morning to you, Jack Pate.*

Now, as he sat across the glass from me, he looked like a beaten man. A shell of the errant knight I had come to know.

He spoke first. "This is the end of the line for me, brother. But you've got your whole life ahead of you. Don't blow it this time."

I didn't know what to say. There was so much I wanted to ask him. How, exactly, had he managed to insinuate himself into my life for all these years, going back well before we ever met face-to-face? He drove the same Land Rover as me, for Christ's sake. Knew where I lived. Where Barbara lived. Claimed to have been at the Olympic Park the same time I was there. Had he managed to lift the note, the note *he* himself had written, from my glove box that time? How had he known I'd been locked up? How had he known I'd be at Emory? All I could assume was that, for twenty years, he had made it his mission, damned near twenty-four-seven, to shadow my every move.

Why had he chosen the path he had? Had he somehow set out to be the Bad Jack to my good? What might he have experienced at the hands of *my* father and *our* mother in his early years, before his banishment to a life of privileged near-neglect, that might explain the man he had become? Why was he so fixated on the Rudolph brothers? On firebombs? On me?

And whatever happened to his stepmother Janice? I never saw any sign of her at the house. Had she been sent away somewhere? Or was she just gone for the day? Or gone period?

So many questions. But something told me it just wasn't the time to bring any of this up. He was going through a lot right now, more than I could ever imagine myself going through. I knew we'd have more opportunities to talk.

But there was one question I had to know the answer to. "Why did you kill Stanley Jacobs? He didn't do anything to hurt you."

David stiffened. "Au contraire, Jack. Remember when I told you about the man in the Ranger who brought me part of the way to your cabin then dropped me off?"

"The *cain't go no further* one?"

"That's the one."

"Well, I lied. Half-lied, actually. You see, that man was Jacobs. And he didn't give *me* a ride anywhere. Fact is, I gave *him* a ride. And it wasn't when you think. It was New Year's Eve."

David went on to say that he had just walked out of the Murphy Save A Lot when Jacobs approached him. "At first, I thought he was just another vagabond, but then I saw the Ranger a few yards away. 'That your truck?' I said. He nodded. He asked if I was going north. I said yes. He told me he had a flat tire without a spare and asked if I would be so kind as to take him to his cabin about halfway between Murphy and Marble."

David said they eased Jacobs' Ranger behind the Save A Lot so it wouldn't get towed away. Then they headed north.

"You were in your Land Rover?"

"I was. You know the one. Just like *yours*."

I told him I had seen it as he sped away from his parents' house in Waco.

He continued. "Somewhere near Tomotla, he had me turn down a dirt road. We came upon a cabin in the woods. Rundown, not like yours. He said, 'Come on in and let's have a drink. It's New Year's Eve after all.' I followed him inside. He pulled out a bottle of Jim Beam, and that was that."

"What do you mean that was that?"

"Well, Jack, you see, we finished off the bottle. Then he opened another. By the time midnight came around, we were both plastered beyond recognition. That's when he decided to pick a fight with me. He became downright belligerent."

"Over what?"

"I don't even know. It was all a blur. What I *do* know is that I grabbed a fireplace poker and went at him. He fell back. His head hit the hearth." David grimaced. "He died, Jack."

"So, it was all an accident."

"It was, but the fire wasn't. As soon as I realized Stanley Jacobs had met his maker, I decided to burn the place down to hide the evidence. And then the oddest thing happened."

"What was that?"

"It felt exhilarating. Liberating. A sense of destiny welled up inside me. I wondered at the time whether, somehow, my newfound calling harkened back to my daddy, your daddy."

"Your *calling*?"

"I told you back in Waco that I always wanted to be somebody. I wanted people to read about me in the paper. Remember when you said I looked like Eric Rudolph, and I said who's that?"

"I remember it. I was shocked you didn't recognize the name."

"Oh. I recognized it alright. Truth be told, I'd been following him, and his brother, from…what's the proletarian expression?…oh yes, from the get-go."

I asked him why, if he had a vehicle all along, he had traveled everywhere on foot.

He laughed. "All a ruse, Jack. I have to tell you, though, I had a blast playing the errant knight."

"But when you first showed up at my cabin that night, you looked like you hadn't bathed in days. And, pardon me for saying it, but a funk was following you."

"What would a good ruse be without the full sensory experience?"

The guard walked over. "You need to wrap it up now, Pate."

David held up his index finger. "One more minute, please."

He returned his attention to me. "You know what, Jack. There's something you need to hear before you go. I'm sure you tried your best to be a good father, but your children were starved for attention. I know what that feels like." A tear coursed down his cheek. "Go back to them, Jack. They need a father." He looked away, then back at me. "I must return to my cell, now. Okay?" He smiled. Bigger than ever. Number 5 sparkled with such intensity that it seemed to wash the space around him with light. "Until next time, my brother."

As I walked from the Polaris to my cabin, I noticed a note tacked to my door. It read YOU'RE A GOOD MAN, JACK. NOW LIVE IT.

The door was unlocked. I walked inside. The first thing I noticed was that the painting was gone.

I lay in bed that night thinking about the complexity of the human heart. At its core often lies a delicate balance, an intricate ballet danced on the fine line between admiration and resentment. Between emulation and jealousy. Between good and bad. And sometimes that delicate balance falls apart. Sometimes the dancer loses his footing and tumbles to the floor. But sometimes, if he's lucky, he picks himself up and makes the best of what his short life on this earth has to offer. And if he's successful, he learns to muzzle the black dog.

25

FAMILY

Saturday morning, the 31st of January.

I pulled into the Abbottsford subdivision before sunup. Barbara's car was in the driveway. The turquoise bike was in the front yard where it had been the last time I was there. A basketball sat at the base of the adjustable backboard waiting patiently for its next opportunity.

I eased the Land Rover along the curb in front of the house. My right front tire grazed the curb's edge. I cut the engine and waited for the lights to come on inside. My heart pounded. I rehearsed what I would say when Barbara realized I had returned. How would she receive me? How much would I tell her about the last month? About my brother? About the black dog? Would she believe me when I said I was, if not a changed man, at least a man committed to doing whatever it took to get help. To have our lives back together?

The first light to come on was in Barbara's bedroom. Then the light in the front bedroom on the other end of the house. I assumed that was Jake's room.

I got out of the car and walked around to the kitchen side of the house, almost tripping over the bike.

The kitchen light was on.

I crept up to the window and peered inside. The winter sun hadn't yet risen, so I assumed I wouldn't be seen.

Jake and Bobbie were sitting at the table. Barbara was at the stove.

I watched as Barbara put breakfast on the table. Scrambled eggs, pancakes, bacon. Just like old times. Then she took the seat across from the kids with her back to the window, and they all dug in.

A vicarious warmth came over me.

Halfway through breakfast, the sun began its ascent over the horizon.

Jake happened to look up. He saw me standing outside the window.

We locked eyes.

He beamed.

I went around to the front door and rang the bell.

Acknowledgments

When I embarked on a second career as a fiction writer, I had no idea how critical three people would be to my success. I met them at a meeting of the Blue Ridge Poets and Writers Guild and, shortly thereafter, I was invited to join their critique group. Glen Heefner, Julia Sennette, and Dru Sumner have taught me to be a better writer and have inspired me to keep at it even during times of self-doubt. I will forever be indebted to them for their guidance and abiding friendship. They have helped me through every chapter, every page, and every word of this book, just as they did with my prior three books.

And while two prior members of the group, John Ripma and the late John Edwards, had no direct hand in *Muzzle the Black Dog*, I am grateful for the impact they had on my prior books.

I owe a huge debt of gratitude to Dea Shandera, my publicist, for her expertise, guidance, and encouragement, and to Joey Madia for graciously reading the advance copy of *Muzzle the Black Dog* and providing meticulous feedback.

Caren, my wife of forty-seven years, has been by my side and provided encouragement every step of the way. She has endured my writing obsession, hours heads-down at my laptop, and personal slights with a smile. She is my soulmate.

I am also indebted to my family and friends who continue to support and encourage my passion for writing.

Much of my work prior to August nineteenth last year was done with our precious Bella by my side or nearby. While she may not have realized it, she provided inspiration beyond measure. She is missed every day. While she was *our* black dog, she was not the inspiration for this book.

Lastly, I would like to thank my characters. Without them, there would be nothing.

About The Author

MIKE COBB'S body of literary work includes both fiction and nonfiction, short-form and long-form, as well as articles and blogs. While he is comfortable playing across a broad range of topics, much of his focus is on true crime, crime fiction and historical fiction. Rigorous research is foundational to his writing. He gets that honestly, having spent much of his professional career as a scientist. He vehemently refuses to box his work into a specific genre.

Mike splits his time between Atlanta and Blue Ridge, Georgia.

MGCOBB.COM

f MGCobbWriter

𝕏 @mgcobb

⌾ cobbmg

About The Type

This book is set in Adobe Caslon, a typeface designed by Carol Twombly and based on William Caslon I's original design dating to the mid 1700s. Caslon, a trained London engraver and typefounder, is widely credited for creating the first original typeface of English origin and establishing a national typographic style. Caslon's self-titled typeface is know for its enduring style and legibility.

In the late 19th century the Caslon typeface was adapted for hot metal typesetting with the gaining popularity of mass-market printing.